Definite

Copyright

Written by Elodie Nowodazkij - Copyeditor: Kael Pryble - Proofreader: Katharen Martin

Cover by Elodie Nowodazkij – Damian and Maddie illustrations by Qamber Emporium

www.elodienowodazkij.com—elodie@elodienowodazkij.com

Book summary

EXCLUSIVE: MADDIE SMITH—NICKNAME: Ice Princess—Melts for Grumpy Hero. Sources Say She's in Denial.

Swans Cove: the small-town where I'm rebuilding my award-winning career, not falling for the tall, tattooed, grumpy ex-bodyguard next door. Damian Mack doesn't trust me, I don't like him, and he's definitely not infuriatingly hot. (Okay, maybe a little.)

My rom-com life took a horror movie turn when my "perfect" proposal went viral—for all the wrong reasons. And here I am: writing feel-good stories, "trying" to charm the locals (well, some of them), and feeling like I'm stuck in pit lane while everyone else is racing by.

But between nosy neighbors and an unwanted attraction that's throwing off my game, my foolproof plan is getting more complicated by the minute.

"Definitely Not Lovers" is my story—a rollercoaster of humor, heart, and heat that I never saw coming. Will I stick to my plan and prove everyone wrong, or will Swans Cove—and Damian—make me reconsider everything?

One thing's for sure, this wasn't part of the plan. Now, what would a winner do?

This is a prequel novel that ends on a cliffhanger... maybe like me, you'll just keep wanting more.

Author's note:

DEAR WONDERFUL READER,

Thank YOU so much for picking up this copy of *Definitely NOT Lovers Damian & Maddie #1*! I've started writing this prequel novel because I needed to know Maddie and Damian before their route to Happily-Ever-After in # Dear Santa, With Love.[1]

I am really so grateful to you as your reviews, word-to-mouth, social media posts (however you decide to share about this book) will help Maddie and Damian travel worldwide!

I'm crossing my fingers that Maddie and Damian's prequel novel makes you smile. It ends on a cliffhanger! <3

If you'd like to show your love to Maddie and Damian, make sure to continue reading their story in # Dear Santa, With Love[2]. And/or join my newsletter[3] (if you haven't already) to get bonus scenes and more.

Thank YOU again so much!

<3

Elodie

www.elodienowodazkij.com[4]

---

1. https://books2read.com/dearsantawithlove
2. https://books2read.com/dearsantawithlove
3. https://subscribepage.io/9EuZte
4. http://www.elodienowodazkij.com

This one is for those of you guarding your heart—for whatever reason. <3

CHAPTER 1—MADDIE

Seven months ago—Valentine's Day

Subject line: Your last article
Dear Maddie, your last article needs more than a bit of rework. An entire rewrite. We've talked about this more than once: you need more emotions in your words.
Connections matter. Don't forget that.
Santos.

PROPOSING TO MY PERFECT Super Bowl-winning boyfriend on Valentine's Day ticks all the boxes of a wonderful story: romantic, perfectly organized, *emotional.* Plus, it fits the plan: married by thirty-five, a Pulitzer Prize by forty, and making my family proud.

Yet, here I am, snow seeping through my so-not-sensible heels at twilight, waiting for Chase, who is—I glance down at my watch—seventeen minutes late.

I'm pretty sure my smile is frozen into a grimace that could rival the clown from Stephen King's *It*. My palms are clammy. My pulse is racing like Lewis Hamilton in the São Paulo Grand

Prix years ago, and my nerves are playing pinball with my heart. The lavender/vanilla essential oils that Becca, my forever best friend, has been spraying for "calm and love" must have stuck to my blazer and my hair. The scent isn't calming. It has me wanting to rush back inside and hide under the heavy comforter, pretending it's a bunker.

But I can't.

Because did I mention the plan?

So what if my shallow inhales and exhales would disappoint yoga teachers around the world? I've got this under control. There's no serial killer creeping in the snow-covered bushes.

This is a proposal—not my favorite true-crime podcast.

"Maddie." My sister says my name like she's been rehearsing a speech. And not a bridesmaid speech. "Are you sure it's the day?"

Yep. Totally sure. Even if Chase's good-morning texts have become a thing of the past. It doesn't mean anything. We're growing, *evolving*. Nothing to worry about. I really should stop nibbling my lower lip—it's not going to be great for my barely-there pinkish lipstick. The one Chase loves.

"Of course, I'm sure. You know me. I've got everything planned down to the minute." My unwavering gaze stares ahead as Hitchcock-worthy crows pick at my ribs, their wings flapping in my chest. And those crows must be rabid and multiplying by the second. But I ignore them because it cannot go wrong. Nothing can go wrong.

My fingers reach out for my necklace—the one I dug out from a pile of knick-knacks under the sign "Love Me Forever" at a vintage store years ago. It reminded me of the necklace my grandfather gave my grandmother. It's a necklace with a story. A love story. But instead of the trusted silver chain, my fingers tap my flushed skin. "Have you seen my necklace?" At least I don't sound like I'm losing my shit. Go, me.

My sister glances around the beautiful winter farm landscape under the twinkling lights, frowning, serious—like she's on a CSI set—fitting since she's auditioned for a new investigative series two weeks ago. "Not since we left. I'm pretty sure it was on your nightstand back in the city."

There's a pang in my chest.

One of my colleagues wrote about those sinkholes forming in the road. Well, there must be one forming deep within me, and pressing my manicured nails into my palms doesn't close it back up.

It's just a necklace. Nothing more. But not feeling its weight on my skin has me wondering if everyone can stare right into my heart and see all my uncertainties, all my hopes, all the ways I'm failing.

Failing? Nope. Definitely not. It's not in my vocabulary. I lift my chin, forcing those feelings way back down. What would a winner do? This is what's important, what matters.

I've got this.

"You could still change your mind," Rose adds with a frown, boring her gaze into mine like she's trying to get through to me. And reminding me that, like me, she loves having the last word.

"I'm not going to," I reply, glaring at her. Becca, who had been trailing behind—to prepare a surprise for our engagement, I'm pretty sure—rushes back to my side.

"She remembered what Chase esaid during an interview about loving surprises," she huffs and puffs, giving me her best you-got-this smile, and I'd hug her if she wasn't holding the ring light for the video set-up.

Rose crosses her arms over her chest. "Fine, but are you doing this because it's what you want, or because you're confusing a good story with a good life?"

"Seriously? Do you think this is one of your soap operas? Is that a line?" My jaw barely unclenches.

"You did pitch it to your editor."

I don't even move an eyebrow. She doesn't need to know this is my last ditch effort to stay at my big New York job after they gave me the feedback my articles were becoming too robotic. My brain is coming up with the best retort when Becca murmurs, "He's here."

And as I spot the impressive frame of my soon-to-be-fiancé, I wait for the rush of endorphins to take over. Endorphins. Adrenaline. Same thing, right?

"Go, go, go." My hands flail in the direction of their hiding spots. Becca gives me a thumbs up and hurries to the bridge nearby, where she'll be able to record the moment. But my sister stays put. Not moving an eighth of an inch.

I groan, "Now, Rose. Goooooooo."

"Fine, but..."

"Just go. He can't see you!"

She sighs dramatically as she finally strides toward the trees behind me—she's going to take pictures from a different angle for the social media campaign I'm planning.

Everything *is* under control.

I focus on the man strolling my way. He's got long-ish hair, and unlike me, he's wearing a hat and a winter coat and... gloves.

Crap. How do I get him to take off the gloves? Or does he take them off after I propose? The ring I bought at my favorite jeweler burns inside my pocket.

I tighten my way-more-fashionable blazer around me and tell myself to stop shaking.

He turns toward the barn, holding what looks to be a lasso—and a tinge of panic tightens around my neck. That's not the plan. He's supposed to meet me here, by the bridge.

"Hey," I whisper, but he doesn't hear me. I call out louder. "Hey." Now I sound like a coach on the sidelines. "Hey," I try again, injecting as much sweetness in my tone as possible, like Rose used to do in her career-defining soap opera role.

He waves my way, but he's not hurrying toward me to shield me from the snow or to give me one of those old-movie-Hollywood kisses that will look great on camera.

I trudge forward.

When I stop in front of him, I force my lips into a hey-babe smile—expecting him to smile back. But he looks away.

"Madison," he says in that deep, serious but warm voice of his that I know has inspired countless online videos. It's an I've-got-something-to-say voice. What if he's about to propose? A jolt of panic rushes through me. That can't happen. I know he has the ring. I didn't tell my sister, but I've seen it and it's gorgeous. There's no way I'd plan something like this if I wasn't sure of his answer.

This is my time.

But when I bend down, my heel slips, and, with a thud, I end up on both knees with my face pretty close to a very impressive bulge I know oh so very well.

Wonderful.

I know how *that* must look on Becca's video.

I stare at his crotch, narrowing my eyes, thinking for a few seconds.

Why am I trying to remember the last time we had sex? And why can't I?

Must have been pre-Superbowl.

I clear my throat to regain control of the situation—maybe this can be the funny prelude to the most romantic moment ever.

Cold invades my bones as another gust of North Pole-like wind slaps my face, likely ruining my perfect hairdo.

"Are you okay?" he asks, extending a hand to help me up.

But I can't accept it, not now.

"Chase Finn Parker," I finally utter, steadying my voice that sounds way too high-pitched.

I look up at him, his out-of-control beard I'd love for him to trim, and those brown eyes that can be fire and tender. Is he growing paler, or is it just the increasing flurry of snow?

"Madison, please stand up," he urges, his voice still calm. He's never been one to lose his cool, especially with me. It's been a smooth relationship: we're compatible; we make sense. It's a rational decision. A good one.

"Please marry me?" I squeak out. Ohmygosh—where did that almost-Elmo voice come from?

"Wait, wait, let me ask again." I inhale deeply, wiping my muddy hand on my light blue blouse. "Will you marry me?"

My breath catches, waiting, already ready to squeal and wrap my arms around him when he says yes.

He shakes his head. "No."

I'm sorry. What?

This doesn't make sense. I grab onto the different possibilities racing through my mind: he didn't hear my question, he's joking, he wants to be the one proposing.

"No, don't ask again?" It's like my investigative journalist voice can't shut up—is it the time to make sure I understand?

He doesn't answer. Instead, he says the words every romcom lover dreads. "We need to talk."

I've read about hearts crashing into the ground. But my heart doesn't crash. It's frozen in place. I attempt to stand back up, because this seems to be a conversation I shouldn't be having with his zipper, but I slide again.

"Chase," I whisper his name—refusing to believe any of this is real. My hand grasps his muscular thigh—the one that won "Top Athlete Thigh" on the Reddit Thighs Community. The same thigh I voted for.

We were named "It-couple" by E! and Hollywood Reporter. We have our own Reddit community *ChaseandMaddie.* Rose may have asked me if I was sure, but hundreds of people have been speculating about the engagement coming soon.

This was supposed to be the culmination of both my personal and professional life.

"Oh, Maddie," he murmurs. But nothing makes sense. Is there another hidden camera somewhere?

"Chase, please, can we just talk about this?" My voice doesn't crack, but before he can respond, there's a thump in the distance and a loud "moo" very close to me. So close, I'm afraid if I turn around, there's going to be a cow looking at my smudged mascara.

"Buttercup, wait!"

Buttercup? That's one of Chase's favorite cows, and then I feel it: a rough tongue across the back of my head, leaving a trail of warm saliva in my carefully styled hair. I let out a yelp of surprise and disgust, frantically wiping at my head with my muddy hands.

"Buttercup!" Chase exclaims, his eyes widening. "She must have escaped. I'm so sorry, Maddie. Let me just..." He wraps the lasso around her like she's a puppy and moves to guide her back towards the barn, his attention fully diverted from my proposal.

I'm still on my knees, stunned, my hair dripping with cow spit, my dirty and wet clothes clinging to my skin, and my heart shattered into a million pieces. Could this moment get any more humiliating?

As if on cue, a loud whistle pierces the air, followed by a boom. Fireworks explode in the sky above us, forming a giant red heart with "Maddie & Chase Forever!" written in the center.

Oh no. Becca.

That must have been her surprise.

Chase shakes his head, muttering, "What the fuck?" as Becca pops out from behind the snow-covered bridge.

"Spiders! Snow spiders!" she shrieks, frantically brushing at her coat. Then she looks up and bites her lip, and I know shit is about to hit the fan... because that's her "I'm-so-sorry" tell.

And am I biting mine, or just trying not to implode right here and there? Becca rushes behind Chase as if he'll protect her from the terrifying insect and peeks out from behind his broad back. "Also, I may have been live instead of recording. I told you I didn't know how to use that new phone. There's like a button here." She presses on something that beeps and winces. "Oh no. What did I do now?"

Forget hot and heavy humiliation—mortification scorches through my every pore. People have seen this? I'm going to be the laughingstock at every cocktail party in Manhattan, and a meme by morning.

"You were filming that?" Chase sounds more than annoyed. He sounds pissed, and he's narrowing his eyes with that posture that tells me I didn't poke the bear—I lit a fire under him.

I ignore his question.

Digging my hands into the snow, I force myself to try to stand up again. Success. My legs shake. Forget a sinkhole, there's an 8.5 magnitude earthquake in my stomach, but instead of curling into a ball and waiting for the aftershocks to roll through, I lunge forward and snatch Becca's phone.

Damage control. I need to do damage control.

"I m-might still be live," she mutters, her eyes wide with panic, but I barely hear her over the roaring in my ears.

"I saw the Tiffany box in your closet! And the ring!" The words burst out, filled with accusation—not only at him, but at myself. Did I get everything wrong? "We've been dating for two years." My gaze darts to the barn, trying to understand. "Is there someone else?" I don't voice the question that's resonating so loudly in my head it hurts, "Am I not enough?"

Instead, I clear my throat and, with one mud-macked hand holding the phone and the other on my waist, I challenge him. "You told me I was the love of your life. Or did you forget?"

Chase holds the cow with one hand, his shoulders tightening before sagging oh so slightly. He looks furious and defeated all at once. "You staged all of this, just like you've staged our entire relationship. I'm just a supporting character in the Madison Smith story. And I can't do it anymore."

Each word feels like a slash of Michael Myers' knife, cutting deeper and deeper into my carefully cultivated image. "But, but the Tiffany box..." My voice is paper-thin.

"It's a marketing gift." His tone softens. "Listen, Maddie. You know it's better this way." His face fills with resignation and pity. And that pity has my blood turning into steam.

"Better?" I snicker—fury storming in my voice. Safer than the pain settling deep inside of me, getting comfortable as if it's ready to order a martini. Chase's favorite drink. The one I taught myself to like.

"Yes. Better." He pauses as if I should understand, and when I shake my head like I'm about to prove to him that it's not better, he adds. "You know I'm just not another trophy to put on your shelf."

Wow. Okay. A bitter laugh claws up my throat, my words dripping with years of knowing exactly what might hurt him. "A trophy? Oh, please. You're not a trophy! You were an experiment, a story. That's it," I spit out. "And a failed one at that."

His eyes narrow, and I hate myself for what I said—but there's no hurt on his face.

No indignation. No surprise.

He expected my reaction—maybe he was even waiting for it, and he doesn't care.

Because what I think doesn't matter.

Becca and Rose are staring at me, their faces mirrors of shock and secondhand embarrassment. And behind them, the fireworks are still bursting in mocking hearts, branding my failure across the night sky.

I've covered enough celebrity breakups fresh out of college to know there's no coming back from this.

No witty soundbite or charming interview can spin this nightmare. For once in my life, I'm speechless.

Chase turns to walk away, his broad shoulders disappearing into the darkness.

And I'm left with the smell of cow saliva and the dying sparks of my shattered dreams.

But I won't let the credits roll on my perfect life.

Even as I blink away the tears that threaten to spill, and shame scorches the back of my throat, I turn to the camera. "And here you have it, another relationship bites the dust. Thanks for watching. Wishing you all much love." I pause, thinking of what word to add. "And happiness." And I stop the live, ignoring the aching in my chest.

That's what a winner would do, right?

CHAPTER 2—DAMIAN

Voicemail: Hiiii, it's Mom! Just checking in on you. Did you read that article I sent you? It's research for my next novel. According to a Pew Study, about 10% of people in the US who are in committed relationships met on a dating app... My editor is calling. Wait. How do I pick it up... Love.... beeeeeeep.

WHOEVER MOVED INTO the apartment upstairs three days ago either has a questionable sense of humor or serious insomnia. I crumple the first pink Post-it I found stuck on the dryer, reminding me about the senior yoga classes at the community center, and toss it into the trash with a frown.

I pluck the second Post-it—yellow, this time with the words: "Thanks for moving your clothes in a timely fashion. It's just best for everyone. And please, let me know if you need help." Except their cursive p is so high up, it meshes with the l, and it looks like whoever penned this wrote *Hell.* I started the wash at three in the morning—it's barely six-thirty.

But apparently, 2A doesn't agree.

The sun barely peeks through the small windows in the laundry area, and a whiff of lavender and vanilla invades my lungs. That scent has been everywhere since the new tenant moved in three days ago, spraying essential oils like a ritual.

As I pull out the warm shirts from the dryer, I groan. "Shit." All the white shirts I ordered for next week's first class of "Go! Seniors" are now pink. And I don't have time to reorder new shirts. My jaw tightens. Fucking perfect. So what if my dentist warned me about grinding my teeth? If it helps me stay in control, I'll shatter all my molars.

I bend down to check the tumble and find something dark red, lacy, and definitely not mine.

Way to go, Grandma. I guess.

I almost slap my own note on the dryer but think better of it. Instead, I shove the panties in my back pocket—I'll confront 2A on my terms.

Not right now.

I've got to work out, check on permits, finalize the marketing plan, and convince Aunt Locelli to join the class. When I first moved in Swans Cove, she overheard me on the phone with my phone (because of she did) and told me to call her Aunt Locelli—despite the fact we're not family. She knows everyone and she knows how to spread the word. If she joins the class, others might follow. And we need them to follow...

This class is my idea. It might help. And 2A won't derail me.

Back in my apartment, I drop the shirts on my bed, pour myself a coffee, and grab my laptop, scanning the latest financial reports. The numbers hit me with more force than the G-force in a Formula One car. Red everywhere. We expanded too fast and took on too much debt. This new senior class isn't just an idea anymore—it's a lifeline. If it fails... I shove that thought into one of my many let's compartmentalize mental boxes and slam the lid.

Failure isn't an option.

My phone buzzes. Alessandro.

"Hey, you see the latest projections?" His voice is tight, stress evident even through the phone.

"Yeah," I grunt. "We need this class to work, Al. And that damn interview better be good PR." My gaze drifts to the window.

A woman is outside, doing some kind of elaborate dance to avoid a bee. She's juggling a phone and a coffee cup and laughing in such a way that I want to be in on the joke. She's got curves like a Ferrari and legs that go on for miles in those high-heel shoes, but I know better than to take that particular model for a test drive.

"It will be," Alessandro says. "But one interview might not cut it. Even with your legendary charm."

I snort. "Ed will be fair."

"About that," Alessandro clears his throat. "It's not Ed. New hire. I'll send you the details when I have them."

"Doesn't matter who it is. I'll handle it." I pause, rubbing the back of my neck. "We've got the Chamber of Commerce meeting next month. We just need to show growth."

The woman's now raising her phone in the air, probably searching for a signal.

"Right," Alessandro says. "Got five people coming for Morning Muscles. Gotta go."

As he hangs up, my eyes drift back to the woman—but she's gone.

Despite my mother's meddling, I'm not on dating apps. And I'm not planning to be. They work off location, and I've got rules about getting involved with locals for a reason. Last thing I need is some grandma trying to set me up with her visiting granddaughter.

I turn away from the window, pulling on my faded black t-shirt and well-worn gray sweatpants. Time to focus on what matters—keeping this business afloat.

My phone rings again, and I frown. Alessandro and I always catch up before the 7 am class, but it's way too early for Aisling to call me. "I need your help." My best friend's fiancée sounds like she's on the verge of a nervous breakdown. And Aisling keeps herself together better than some hard-ass Navy Seals.

"What's happening?" I balance my phone against one ear as I check our work inbox.

"Well..." She clears her throat. "Sorcha was supposed to volunteer in Ava's class today, but she's out with a stomach bug, and I can't leave the bakery, and Alessandro is only coming back after lunch and..."

"And you don't want Ava to be disappointed."

"Exactly." I can almost hear the wince in her voice. "I know we're asking a lot. Between the interview this afternoon and now this... if it's too much, don't worry. Also, it's early. I'm calling too early, right?"

I can see Aisling now, probably wearing a path into her kitchen floor.

Knowing she's worried makes me want to spring into action. "Ava's school? What time do you need me to be there?"

"Nine? I swear I'll bake cupcakes and cakes and everything your heart desires."

"A carrot cake with caramel icing?"

"You got it." Aisling sounds relieved. She's the type that hates asking for help. She's gotten better at it, and she usually doesn't hesitate if it's to ensure Ava isn't disappointed.

"I'll be there."

"Thank you!"

Once she hangs up, I go through most of my early morning to-do list, including some cardio and boxing, to release some of the tension before heading to the elementary school. Despite being way past Labor Day, the air has that Maryland heaviness to it: hot and humid with that salty ocean scent that I love.

As soon as I walk in and scribble my name on the sign-in sheet, the assistant leads me to the community room. The room's a zoo of high-pitched squeals and chatter. Oh, man.

And apparently, I'm supposed to lead a... hold up, a drawing class? With pencils and paints and glitter and—is that a freaking crown?

Ah, what the hell. I plop the plastic crown onto my head and give the laughing kids a dramatic bow. Might as well lean into it, right?

"Thank you so much for coming," Ava's teacher says, batting her eyelashes at me.

She's made it plenty clear that I'm welcome to swing by her place anytime to check out her "amazing fish tank." But despite that gorgeous ass and come-hither smile, I've never taken her up on it. I know how to pour on the charm without making promises I don't intend to keep.

"I'm so glad you're able to come to our show and tell for our art class," she gushes.

Art class. Fan-fucking-tastic. The only time I pick up a brush is during PTSD meetings with the guys, and that shit's not exactly finger-painting material.

"Uncle Damian!" Ava's voice slices through the chaos, her little hand waving like she's hailing a taxi. Hearing this pint-sized kiddo call me "Uncle Damian" like I'm actually family... it wraps around my heart tighter than a tactical vest. They chose me. I chose them. No way in hell I'm letting her down.

"Why do you look so sad?" Ava asks, tugging me toward a table that looks like Michaels threw up on it. Mini canvases everywhere, and one big one that Sorcha probably planned to use for some actual art lessons.

Me? I'm pretty sure if I busted out my brand of "art," Ava's teacher would need a defibrillator. Definitely not PG. Hell, not even R-rated.

I slap on my best everything's-cool grin for Ava. "I don't look sad." But she narrows her eyes, suspicion written all over her face. She looks so much like Alessandro, it's eerie. Blood doesn't make family—I know that better than most. Alessandro wears that "Dad" title like a medal of honor, and it's something not to take for granted.

“Well,” Ava declares, marching up to the big canvas like a tiny general. “I can show you how to draw a dog.” The other kids gather around her, ready for some guidance. Which is a damn good thing, because me trying to teach art? That's a recipe for disaster. Unless you count stick figure ninja moves as art. And X-rated drawings.

I could teach some confidence moves. I could make it fun. And silly.

Hey, maybe we should start a "Have Fun and Be You" class for kids. Could be onto something there.

"Are you listening to me, Uncle Damian?" Ava's voice snaps me out of my thoughts.

"Sure thing, baby girl."

"I'm not a baby," she huffs, just as one of the kids smears paint on another's head.

Ah, shit. I jump in to do some damage control, guiding the little paint-covered Picasso to the sink, letting the water run through my fingers to make sure it's not too hot or too cold.

Once the crisis is averted, I settle in to watch Ava's lesson, hunching my shoulders to make my bulky frame a little less imposing. And you know what? The dog in my painting actually looks like a dog. Not too shabby.

Ava sidles up to me, studying my work. "You smile like our doggie," she says, and I can't help but puff up a bit. Their dog is one smart, lovable, stubborn son of a gun.

But then Ava tilts her head, her next words hitting me square where I've got scars from a tour gone wrong: "But sometimes, like him, you have sad eyes."

Damn. Leave it to a kid to see right through me, to all the parts I try to keep hidden away.

A FEW HOURS LATER, after scoffing down one of Plates & Drinks' best cheese-melting Cuban paninis for a way-too-late lunch, I step into the dog shelter, the familiar scent of wet fur and kibble filling my nostrils. It's an oddly comforting smell, mixed with the sound of excited barks and the clatter of claws against concrete. The humidity clings to my skin, but the pure joy radiating from these dogs makes it all worthwhile.

I've been volunteering at the shelter for the past few months, ever since Alessandro and I stayed in Swans Cove after our stint on the reality TV show *Sweets for Love*. After the Navy, Alessandro was like family, and building a business together made sense. The shelter has become a weekly ritual, a way to give back and find a sense of purpose outside of my work at the self-defense school.

Barkey bounds up to me, his tail wagging so hard his whole body shakes. I crouch down to his level, my muscles protesting slightly from the morning's workout.

"Hey there, buddy," I murmur, ruffling his ears. "Ready to play?" There's nothing like a dog in a shelter finally opening up. Like Barkey here. He's been so down since he arrived, and today, he finally wagged his tail when I stepped into the dog room. I'd say it's my irresistible charm, but all I brought was an old ball, and this dog loves to play fetch. *Loves* it.

I get why he was wary at first, but showing his personality—especially such a fun one—should help him in getting adopted. Even though he's older than the adorable puppies people go for. Shit, I get this dog. More than I'd like to admit.

I rub the back of my neck as I throw the ball again—no need to go down memory lane.

"Again?" I ask Barkey as he rushes back to me with the ball that's basically turned wet from his drool. His nose presses against my hand, and he's looking at me with eyes that make me want to fill out the adoption papers. But I can't. Not yet, at least. Paul has reservations about dogs over 20 lbs. in the building. I have a meeting planned with him to discuss those restrictions.

After another half an hour, my watch beeps with a message from Alessandro, and I frown when I realize the time.

Hey, I know Aisling reminded you about the interview. It's still at 3 pm. But Aisling hasn't seen you. You think you can make it?

Shit, it's almost 3 pm. And while Swans Cove is pint-sized, I still need at least ten minutes. And I smell like dogs.

Oh well.

Getting my phone from my back pocket, I call my boss and best friend. "I know I'm the most charming of the both of us—but remind me why I'm doing an interview? Ryan's ankle is almost healed—we'll get the customers back. And everyone knows us."

I rub the back of my neck as I balance the ball and throw it to Barkey. This dog can run fast even in this humidity. I need to make sure I add this to his profile—and maybe Sorcha could add a cute hat on his head for his adoption page. Something with the words "I love to sprint." Maybe he'd be great for someone who's looking for a companion who can jog with them.

"Because you're starting that Senior Self-Defense and Mobility class, and that will be great marketing. Plus, you know that you're usually the life of the party..." His voice trails off, and I can almost picture him wincing. "And I really didn't want to be featured on their one-on-one. That reporter is new, comes from the city, and they're probably going to ask about the TV show and my brother. I mean, we're cool and all, but I thought..."

I get it, so I use my trademark humor to ease the atmosphere. "And I'm better-looking, I get it. Did you pick the bakery as a meeting spot?"

"No, she did."

So, she's indeed probably one of those reporters who are hoping to get a glimpse of Alessandro and Aisling. I clench my jaw. They both are private people despite their relative fame.

"And the name of the reporter?"

"Madison Smith." He lowers his voice. "Ed just sent it to me... I didn't know until now. She was a byline on that article about security bodyguards."

Fucking wonderful.

That article had shed an important light on certain issues like the lack of certification and thorough background checks—but also had lumped Alessandro's former business into it, without using the quote we had given.

My jaw clenches again.

"Okay. I'm on my way."

I can't wait to meet Big City Reporter.

As I head to the bakery, my mind races with everything riding on this interview. The expansion, the loans, the new programs we've poured everything into. We need this publicity, need it to be positive. I clench my fists, steeling myself. I have to make this work. I have to present our business in the best light possible.

Even if we've had shitty experiences in the past with articles gone wrong.

CHAPTER 3—MADDIE

Subject line: Hired.
Dear Ms. Smith, it was a pleasure chatting with you about local news—and we're pleased to offer you the short-term assignment. Looking forward to welcoming you in Swans Cove—one of Maryland's most charming small towns.
Ed

"ALRIGHT, SWANS COVE... here I come," I murmur to myself, squinting at the sun-drenched quaint street. I don't have time to go home, take a shower, and change—because being late isn't an option. So, I readjust my blouse that's starting to stick to my sweat-damp skin the best I can, and my hair (can it be any frizzier?). The bell rings as I step inside the bakery/café, and the aroma of freshly baked cupcakes and cinnamon rolls has my stomach grumbling. A gust of much-needed A/C swirls in the air, making me shiver, but I welcome the goosebumps.

Let's just say that even in the late summer, Maryland is even more humid than I thought. It's like walking straight into a soup—a soup seasoned with Old Bay. A crab soup, really.

I never realized how much Old Bay one could add to everything until I moved here. Fries? Old Bay. Shrimp? Old Bay. Toast with butter? Old Bay.

"Sorry, hun," an older lady tells me as she strolls past me to grab one of the books on the bookshelf by the large windows. I know that author... she started in fanfiction, and I spent hours devouring her Cold Case Detectives stories.

Julie Simmons.

She's married to the billionaire Landon Adams. They have a house here by the water.

I even wrote an article about all the changes Julie had made behind the scenes at the Books For All Foundation, helping distribute books. When I tried to move into more personal stories, I was reminded my place was more in research. Oh, I showed my former boss and the world that I could write personal stories...

Except when he asked me to write about my failed proposal, I couldn't.

"She's the new reporter," I overhear someone whispering, and I square my shoulders, giving the ladies at the table nearby a smile. It may be tight, but it's there.

I'm determined to rise from the ashes of humiliation. Seven months of rebuilding, and I'm ready to prove I'm more than a viral moment or a failed relationship. This interview is my chance to show I'm still capable, still valuable. It's temporary, but it could be the stepping stone I need.

"Did you see the video?" Someone chuckles. And maybe they're talking about some other viral video.

The clock above the door tells me I still have a few minutes, so I walk to the bookshelf.

The framed wedding veil on the top shelf catches my eye, and my chest tightens. It's been months since the epic failed proposal, but the memory still makes breathing in public feel like a Herculean task. That meltdown where I blamed everyone, including myself... because it was my fault. All of it. I inhale deeply, forcing the thoughts away. I can't let that define me anymore.

I focus on the designer's signature in the frame: Sorcha O'Connor. I heard about her. She also went viral after being humiliated, but I'm pretty sure she didn't lose her crap on everyone around her. Maybe we should form a support group.

Social media is still a minefield, but I'm learning to navigate it carefully. I know what to post—but I don't want people to think I'm trying too hard. My phone beeps, jolting me back to the present. Five minutes until the interview. If this goes well, maybe those lukewarm 'maybe another day' responses will turn into enthusiastic yeses.

I can write feel-good, and sugary and sweet. Like those cupcakes staring at me as I inch toward the counter.

The woman standing behind the delicious-looking pastries smiles at me. Sorcha's sister: Aisling O'Connor. I saw her on *Sweets for Love,* and wow, her and Alessandro Torre made me believe in love.

"I want all of the cupcakes." A voice behind me startles me. Is that little boy speaking to me? He frowns. "Are you going to buy all the cupcakes for yourself?"

And before I can answer, his eyes crinkle, and he wails. "Daaaaaaaaaaaaaads, the lady is going to be buying all the cupcakes."

I glance back toward the couple standing behind me. Both men look exhausted but happy. One of them lifts his hand. "Don't worry about him. He's got this cupcake thing right now, but he knows he's only allowed one. We're sorry."

"I get it. They look scrumptious."

I smile back at them, feeling like maybe this small-town gig is exactly what I needed after all. The perfect fresh start, until one of them, who looks like he could be a football player, gives me that look that tells me he's seen me before but can't quite place me.

I whirl back around before the confused question can be asked. *"Have we met before?"*

No, no, we haven't, but if I sat next to a cow, with my mascara running down my face, with a Superbowl champion next to me, you'd probably remember me.

It's either that or the meltdown afterward. I wasn't able to write. I couldn't concentrate. Failing wasn't in my vocabulary. Or so I thought.

I shuffle forward. "Can I please have an iced latte macchiato and a carrot cake cupcake with the caramel icing, please?"

"Sure thing."

I usually take my coffee without sugar and with oat milk, but right now, I feel like I need a burst of energy and sweetness.

After paying, I settle at an empty table, letting the buzz of the conversations and laughter fade into the distance. My sole focus is on the interview with Damian. No Last Name. It was supposed to be with Alessandro Torre, but I got a text less than ten minutes ago of the change. And a quick online sleuthing session confirmed he's a ghost on social media. Great.

His profile on the self-defense school website is missing a picture. But, I did find a couple of articles on their expansion to pop-up classes in Ocean City and invest in the community. They're growing fast.

The perfect first article for the series.

This one-on-one column was my idea—a chance to shine. As a newcomer in town, I can offer something fresh. But where is he? I scan the place, feeling that same fault line in my stomach crackling. I square my shoulders and replay the questions in my head.

"Madison, right?" His voice startles me. I look up and up... and up. The man towering over me is tall, with a build like an athlete—broad shoulders and a rugged presence. His hair, a cross between dirty blond and light brown, compliments his deep-set green eyes. And his half-grin? He's got that half-grin that I swear must come in the manual of "how to be infuriatingly sexy without trying too hard." Or maybe he wrote it. He's got a small plate with the same cupcake as me in one of his hands and what looks like a hot chocolate in the other one.

"M-Maddie," I correct him, my name jumping out like the first time I watched *Halloween* and nearly leapt off the couch, my heart pounding. But unlike that night, I don't hide behind the covers. Oh no, I keep my eyes trained on him and extend my hand. This is a business meeting. Not a meet-cute. He sets his small plate and drink on the spot in front of me before shaking my hand. And as his strong, calloused hand engulfs mine, electricity jolts through my veins. The alarm blaring in my mind resonates through my entire body. He's a live wire, reminding me that behind the façade, the romance in my books doesn't seem to fulfill all my... needs.

Maybe I just need a new vibrator.

Connection may seem good on paper, but in reality, it can be deadly.

"I'm Damian Mack," he rasps out and stares at me like he's waiting for me to say something important.

"Nice to meet you. And thank you for agreeing to take over Alessandro's interview. I really appreciate it."

And I guess I didn't crush whatever exam he was giving me because he frowns.

"I don't have much time for this," he states abruptly, sitting down. And there goes my warm buzz. The way he dismisses *this*—my opportunity to prove to the Swans Cove Gazette that I can weave humor, relevance, and heart into my writing—cuts right into my gushing scars. The ones I hide under my makeup. and my hard work. and my computer.

He then offers a warm smile to someone walking by. So, he *is* capable of friendliness, just seemingly not with me.

Maybe he knows who I am and has decided I'm not worth his time. He wouldn't be the first.

It seems that the lump in my throat has sharp edges now, but I refuse to let it derail me.

Because he's wrong.

And I'm going to prove it.

CHAPTER 4—DAMIAN

Alessandro: Love the pic with the crown Ava's teacher posted on the school forum today. Man, watching you right now: you look pissed. Remember... she's supposed to love us.

THANK YOU, SWANS COVE, for being a small town and giving me a short distraction from the woman sitting in front of me who acted like she didn't recognize my name.

When Aunt Locelli strolls by us with a coffee in hand, I wave at her with my most charming smile, finally out of the minefield created by Madison Smith that should come with a "Danger Zone" label.

I'm not sure if it's my winning half-grin or the fact Aunt Locelli never strays away from chatting, but she grinds to a stop with eyes filled with questions and gossip. "Hi Damian... how lovely to see you. And you must be Madison Smith."

"Maddie," the woman says again as if saying her full name is some kind of line we shouldn't cross. And talking about rules, I should have had mine stamped somewhere to remind myself of them—because Madison's voice is warm and throaty and has me staring at her a few seconds too long.

Madison Smith with her wavy hair that kisses her chin, a mysterious scar under her eyebrow, and a rose tattoo on her neck. Red lips, hazel eyes, and curves for days. Manicured navy nails that I definitely don't imagine trailing down my back. Nope. Not at all.

I clench my jaw. Madison Smith is a goddamn powder keg, and why does it feel like I'm the idiot with matches?

Aunt Locelli continues, "Welcome to Swans Cove. I saw you joined our residents' group already. We love seeing new faces... " She pauses, glancing from Madison to me. "Are you interviewing Damian for your new column?"

Maddie's eyes narrow for a split second. "How did you know?"

"Oh, hun, I know everything. And I find it so cute that you start by interviewing your neighbor."

"Neighbor?" We both utter at the same time, staring at each other before breaking eye contact as if the heat between us could ignite a blaze.

"Neighbor," I mutter again, my eyes glancing back to her flowy blouse, recognizing the woman I saw this morning dancing to escape a bee so close to my building. And now that she's up close and personal, I remember where else I saw that blouse. Hanging in the laundry area at three in the morning. And I don't believe in coincidence. This isn't one of my mom's romance novels where I'm only going to find out she's my neighbor when I run into her without a shirt on while she's wearing a pink towel.

Madison Smith is my very annoying neighbor with the essential oils and that sexy scrap of fabric as underwear.

Fucking terrific.

Aunt Locelli leans forward, her dimples telling me she's about to share some of her Locelli-signed wisdom. Her voice drops to almost a murmur. "I'm sure it hasn't been easy for you, hun, with all that noise about your failed proposal. I saw that video. It was... something."

Something like vulnerability crosses Madison's face. It's only a split second, but it has me wondering what Aunt Locelli is talking about—until she continues, "Chase, was it?" Her eyes brim with sympathy. "Must have been hard, having it all play out so publicly."

"Failed proposal," I mutter, the pieces falling into place.

That's why the rose tattoo on her neck seems familiar—and the way she purses her lips, too. And that voice? I heard that voice countless times scrolling on social media before I deleted all of them... it was in Reels and TikToks. People stitching and creating their own scenario to her voiceover: "You were just an experiment." She was with Chase Parker, the football player—using him for her own career, playing on his feelings like they didn't matter.

My gaze narrows in on Madison, who's clearly forcing a smile now. It doesn't reach her eyes, and her cheeks are turning red. Yet her voice is poised when she replies, "It was a learning experience. Thanks, Mrs...."

"Oh, call me Aunt Locelli, everyone does." She winks my way. "And don't worry, hun, we're all for second chances here, right, Damian?"

"If you say so," I reply. Because, sure. Second chances. I've seen Swans Cove give second... and sometimes third chances, but to people they consider family. People who've earned their trust, not some big city hotshot looking to make a quick buck off their quaint charm.

This town, these people—they're not just a backdrop for some redemption tour. They're my home, my family. The ones who embraced me and Alessandro when we moved in. I'll be damned if I let anyone, even a pretty reporter with killer curves, use them as fodder for a puff piece.

Maddie shifts in her seat, her eyes darting away from Aunt Locelli's knowing gaze. I can almost see the gears turning in her head, wondering how much more truth the older woman is able to dish out.

"Well, don't you worry, dear. We've all had our hearts broken. But I have a feeling your luck is about to change." She winks at us before sauntering off, leaving me to puzzle over her cryptic words.

"Neighbor, huh?" I lean back in my chair. She's the one who wrote me those notes on the washing machine. Between that, her experiment with someone she was willing to marry, and that article she wrote years ago? My bullshit radar hasn't been activated; it's screaming DEFCON 1.

"I guess, uh, should we get started?" She asks like she doesn't want to dwell on anything Aunt Locelli spilled. And when she looks up at me, I swear her flushing is extending to her neck.

I tap my fingers on the table and drink another sip of my hot chocolate. The bell above the door jingles, signaling the arrival of more customers. The rich aroma of freshly brewed coffee mingles with the sweet scent of baked goods, creating a warm and inviting atmosphere. It's the kind of place that makes you want to sit and stay awhile, even if you've got a million things on your to-do list.

And I do. Including this stupid interview. I clench my jaw, reminding myself this interview isn't just about me or the school anymore. It's about our expansion, the loans, the new programs we've poured everything into. We need this publicity to be positive.

"Sure," I reply, and as I reach for a napkin on the table, she reaches for her recorder. Our hands brush, and a jolt of electricity shoots through me. I inhale sharply, my skin tingling from the brief contact.

Madison snatches her hand away, her cheeks still red. For a moment, our eyes lock, and I see my own surprise and desire mirrored in her gaze.

I lean back in my chair, my heart pounding, trying to ignore the heat coursing through my veins. I can't let myself get distracted. Not now. Not by her.

Yet, there's something about Madison that makes me pause. The flicker of uncertainty in her eyes as she plays around with her recorder, muttering something when it doesn't seem to turn on—tucking a strand of hair behind her ear. It reminds me of the shelter dogs. All bravado on the outside, hiding the hurt underneath.

Shit. What did Aisling put in this hot chocolate?

"I'm sorry. The recorder isn't working the way I want it to. I'll use my phone. Is that okay?"

"Sure," I rasp out again.

"Great." She smiles at me, and I clench my jaw, fighting the urge to return her smile.

I wonder if Madison even realizes the shitstorm she caused, the damage her words did. Or if she just moved on to the next story, leaving us to clean up the mess. And will she do it again? Right when we need people to get to know us. The real us.

I take another bite of the cupcake, focusing on the sweetness and spice.

I've faced tougher challenges than pure attraction to the wrong woman.

Hell, I've pushed my body to the brink during SEAL training, every muscle screaming and begging for mercy. I've jumped from helicopters in HAHO operations more times than I can count, my heart pounding in my ears like a damn jackhammer. And now? I'm fighting to keep our business afloat after an overly ambitious expansion. I know what it means to stay laser-focused, to keep my eye on the target no matter what.

I'll do the interview. For the business. For Alessandro. For everyone counting on us.

But I won't let my guard down.

Madison Smith might be my neighbor, but that doesn't mean I have to trust her.

Time to get this over with.

CHAPTER 5—MADDIE

Subject line: Swans Cove Portrait
Hey Maddie, got another email rejecting the appointment for the portrait. If it goes well with Damian, it might help others begin to trust you more. You know, trust is important in this job.
Ed

OKAY, SO THIS MAN IS officially the inspiration behind all the villains in my favorite romance novels. The ones written by the Great Lady Grey. Magnetically masculine with those broad shoulders and tattoos and scars on his rugged face. Annoyingly charismatic with those laugh lines around his come-get-lost-in-me-green eyes (none of those smiles will ever be directed at me, it seems). And infuriatingly inscrutable with those grunty answers that are like pulling all wisdom teeth out at once without any anesthesia.

Except, unlike Lady Grey's latest deliciously dark-ish hockey steamy romcoms, he's not morally grey and definitely not going to win my heart. I don't think he wants it, unless it's to crush it.

Annoyance radiates from him. That and silence.

I tap my fingers on the table, forcing myself to take a deep inhale. Even the sweet scent of the bakery (the fresh scones Aisling just brought out from the back have a vanilla fragrance that has me wanting to get up and get one) doesn't calm the tension ramping in my mind, my chest, my hard-earned resolve. It feels like Jason, Michael Myers, Ghostface, and heck, even Freddy are whispering my name in the dark—waiting for me to mess up so they can snatch me up.

Maybe it's time to stop falling asleep to scary movies or using true crime podcasts as my lullaby.

From now on, Formula One replays will be my goodnight music.

I write down a few more notes—using that moment to gather my thoughts. The abbreviation for this interview is HIPO*: Hellish Interview Part One.*

As I glance back up, I can't help but notice the tension in Damian's shoulders, the way his eyes keep darting to his phone. Is he worried about something beyond this interview? The article I read about their recent expansion mentioned the competition in Annapolis—maybe things aren't going as smoothly as planned.

"Are we done?" Damian finally asks, like he's both relieved and slightly confused.

I clear my throat. "No, no. Not done. I didn't ask you anything yet." I press on my phone's recording. "You're still relatively new. What is the one thing you'd tell a newcomer about Swans Cove?"

"I thought we were going to talk about the school. Our "Be You: Self-Defense and Mobility" school." He's watching me, like not-blinking watching me. And I resist the need deep within that urges me to sit straighter, to show him he doesn't have any effect on me, that I'm in control. His eyes focus on the folder on the table, and as I glance down, I want to wince. Because it includes a headline analysis of what has been written about Swans Cove in the past year—a lot of those headlines were from gossip websites about Ryan Sawyer and Sorcha O'Connor, and Aisling and Alessandro.

"Well, this series is more about the individuals behind the school. It's not about the school per se. I'll probably mention it, but it's really about you."

And it looks like he just swallowed anchovies mixed with sewage water.

"Hm," he grunts.

"The one thing about Swans Cove?" I probe the man in front of me again, whose jaw is now clenching so hard I can see his muscle tick.

"Trust," he growls. "Crucial."

Trust. Crucial? Who is he? The Yoda of small towns?

And then, as if he's convincing himself he's supposed to be talking, he adds, "It's a tight-knit community. People trust each other."

Why does it sound like an accusation in his mouth?

I take a sip of my iced coffee, letting the sweet taste ground me. Interviews haven't always been my strong suit, but I've worked on it. This is not some sort of ambush, it's a getting-to-know-each-other article. I sigh, keeping my polite smile on my face. I mastered the art of polite smiling. I'd win a gold medal if that was an Olympic sport.

"If I understand correctly, trust plays a big part in Swans Cove." I pause, gathering my thoughts, throwing the script I had in place into the Old Bay-scented wind because this back and forth isn't working. I try a different approach. "What was your first day like in Swans Cove?"

"Messy."

"Messy?" I tilt my head, hoping that it's encouraging him to continue and not showing him that my legendary patience is barely holding by the barbwire tightening around my chest. Maybe he's one of those guys who are blaming the repercussions of the failed proposal on me. After all, Chase is thinking about quitting football. But yes, let's say it's my fault he's probably going to retire after this season and not the fact that his body has taken a beating through the years on the field. Plus, I heard he's happy now.

"Definitely messy."

I wait one, two, three seconds for him to add anything, but the only sounds are the laughter and happy chatter of the people sitting around us.

"How about we play a little game?" I continue when he nods, even if his nod seems more challenging than understanding. "I'm going to give you words, and you just do an association with Swans Cove. Like for me... if you told me..."

"Lies," he grunts, interrupting me.

"Boring." I smile. "There's nothing boring about Swans Cove. And those who say small towns are dull are either lying or definitely don't know what they're talking about." I raise an eyebrow and, without waiting a beat, blurt out. "Okay, so let's do this. I tell you one to two words, and you tell me what you associate that word with in Swans Cove. First one: Favorite place."

Is there hesitation crossing his rugged, handsome face?

He murmurs so low I can barely hear him, "Wouldn't you like to know?"

Is he joking? Maybe he is because he adds louder this time, "The shelter."

I make a mental note to ask him more about this later. That might be the start of a great article.

"Favorite drink?"

"Hot chocolate."

"Pastries."

"Aisling's."

"Food."

"Panini."

"Vanilla."

"Sex." He pauses. "Not my favorite kind."

I almost choke on the next word. Especially since his eyes have darkened and his gaze has dropped to my lips before slowly, oh-so-slowly sliding back up. Is my breath catching in my throat? And why, oh, why, does hearing him say the word "sex" have warmth rising up to my neck and my cheeks? Don't look at his strong hands, Maddie. Don't... too late. There's something about the hands of a man, especially the one sitting right in front of me. They're large, calloused hands, and they currently have me wishing to turn into the mug he's holding. Nope. I'm not thinking about how those hands would feel on my skin. Not at all.

I clear my throat. "Sport."

"Formula One."

My eyes widen slightly, and he's like one of those private detectives I shadowed once—aware of every little detail because he's the one who asks the next question as if I'm the one being interviewed.

Those green eyes don't reveal anything.

"Favorite Grand Prix?" His voice is almost neutral—but I detect the challenge underneath it. He's not asking to get to know me. Oh no, he's testing me.

Challenge accepted, Mr. Tall, Tattooed and Grumpy.

"Monaco." I pause. "Closely followed by Montreal. Yours?"

"Monaco." He bites out as if agreeing with me leaves a sour taste in his mouth. "Who was Mr. Monaco?"

"Graham Hill—even though Ayrton Senna won more times than him."

He leans back in his chair, a ghost of a smile playing on those tempting lips of his. And I'm bracing myself for a technical question, or maybe drivers' stats. If he asks about Lewis Hamilton, he's going to be surprised how well I can answer all those questions. "What did Gehrard put in Senna's room?"

My hand slaps on the table. "Fifty frogs!" Some heads turn toward us, and I lower my voice, "And based on what he said, a snake. My turn." I need to move back to the subject at hand, and Damian nods as if I earned a couple more minutes of his time with this little quiz. "Favorite restaurant?"

"Plates & Drinks. They not only make the best panini, but the farm-to-table food is absolutely delicious."

We're finally getting somewhere.

He takes a sip of his hot chocolate. Who drinks hot chocolate on a hot fall day? And yes, now I'm thinking how a hot chocolate, all smooth and decadent, would have been even better, but it doesn't matter. And he leans back. "It wasn't my plan to move here," he finally says. "But it worked out. This place is peaceful. It has good people." Why do I have the feeling he doesn't count me in that group?

"So, you're saying you weren't planning on staying in Swans Cove; it just happened?"

As I lean in to hear his answer over the buzz of the cafe, Damian's eyes flick down to my lips again, his own parting slightly. For a moment, I forget how to breathe; my heart doing a complicated gymnastics routine in my chest. Get it together, Maddie. He's just a ridiculously attractive man, not a Greek god, even if his biceps might beg to differ.

"Yep," he growls.

Great. We're back to one-syllable answers. He crosses his muscular arms over his chest. At this stage, I'm half-expecting him to storm away without another word. A tornado ready to unleash on the idyllic small town and swipe me away to Oz.

Clearly, I need more sleep. But the man in front of me, who apparently lives in the apartment below, has a tendency to blast music late in the evening. I even resorted to using earbuds for my movies and podcasts. Tonight, I'm knocking on his door. It's not like he's going to open without a shirt on and that raspy voice asking me to come in.

But right now? Right now, I need to set up some rules here in this charming bakery with Mr. Grump in front of me.

"You didn't want to do this interview, did you?" I turn off the recording on my phone and mirror his position.

"Nope."

"Okay. Well, we don't have to do it." I wince. Sure, I can find another topic to write about and make it engaging, funny, and heartwarming within hours. Let's face it: making this man in front of me heartwarming is mission impossible anyway.

"Oh, we do."

I narrow my eyes and lean forward, not yet seething because I'm a professional, but close to it. "So, you're telling me that you want to do this interview after all? Because I understand it can be awkward to talk to a stranger, but when I asked you, "What's your favorite place in Swans Cove?" you grunted, and I think you said, "Wouldn't you like to know?" before answering the shelter."

There's a hint of something else on his face (could it be humor?), and for some reason, I hesitate between bursting out laughing and rolling my eyes so hard they jump out and land on the wall behind us.

But that wouldn't be helpful, would it now?

"Uncle Damian!" A little girl rushes toward us, and the man in front of me transforms from a grunty caveman to an image that speaks directly to my ovaries... smiling, sweet, sincere.

She's got reddish hair and a notepad with her. "Look, look, I drew you!"

The picture she pushes in front of him is one of Superman. "That's because Sandro told me you saved him." She gives me a glance and whispers, "More than once."

Okay, so the man is a hero. A grumpy hero. But still... people are made of layers. And my job is to peel some of them with care and compassion. Not with my teeth. Wait... where did that come from?

"It's a beautiful drawing," I tell the little girl, and the way Damian's entire face turns into stone? It's sending me more warnings than if he had told me to piss off.

But the little girl—Ava—I recognize her from the show inches toward me. She's Aisling's daughter.

"Those are beautiful earrings," she tells me, and this time, it's my turn to smile. Unguarded.

"Thank you so much. I made them."

"You did?"

I nod. "Yep."

"I draw." She pushes the drawing in front of me. "Maybe I could draw you?"

Alessandro—the man who's inspired fanfiction after that stunt he pulled on national TV—marches toward us. "So sorry, she saw Damian, and she had to come say hi." He extends his hand to me, and I stand up. As I do though, the table wobbles, and my leftover coffee spills. Right onto Ava's drawing.

"Oh no. I'm so sorry," I blurt out.

As both Damian and I reach for the napkins to clean up the spilled coffee, our hands brush. And for the second time, those warm and strong fingers send a jolt of electricity up my arm. Our eyes meet, and for a split second, I see my own concern for Ava reflected in his gaze. He might be a grump, but apparently, he's got a soft spot for kids. Noted.

I lower myself to Ava's height. "I'm really sorry. This is a beautiful drawing and..."

Ava's lower lip wobbles, and I swear my heart cracks at the sight, but then Alessandro whispers something in the little girl's ear that has her nodding.

"It is okay to be sad," Ava tells me like she's both reassuring me and her, and wow, feelings overload... Because it's like the past months have been hitting me like a freight train: the breakup, the firing, the move. I've not allowed myself to be sad. To feel all the feelings, and this pint size of adorable and wisdom is right. But it's not the moment for all those emotions to swirl in my chest.

And yet...

Oversized lump forming in my throat? Check. Eyes stinging? Check. Heart pounding in my ears? Check.

Ava turns back to Damian. "You know how good I can draw." She glances from me to Damian. "I taught him and my entire class to draw a dog this morning, and he was wearing a crown, and he made sure no one cried, even after Taylor got paint in her hair." She inhales as if catching her breath before continuing, "Maybe I can draw you and your love."

"Love?" I croak out like a morning frog.

Damian's surprised and slightly harsh chuckle is a crash back to reality. "Oh, she's not my love, honey. She's a reporter."

"Is that a bad word?" Ava asks, and I shake my head.

"No, sweetie. It's not a bad word." I pause. "But apparently, it's a complicated one for Superman."

"How about we let those two finish their interview, sweetie pie." Alessandro smiles at Ava before giving a pointed look toward the man in front of me.

As soon as they're out of earshot, I gather my things. "Listen. Clearly, you're not in the mood or headspace for this. Maybe you're one of Chase's rabid fans?"

He tilts his head like for a split second, I actually confused him.

"Chase?" My voice rises slightly. "Remember. Failed proposal." I tick off one finger after the other. "Tight end? Superbowl champion. Nevermind." There's something akin to recognition in his eyes, and I wish I could turn back time because I've just given him more ammunition against me. "We can reschedule, or I can..."

"No, that's okay. I'll answer your questions. Just make sure you don't misquote me or forget to quote me." He pauses. "Again."

"What does that mean 'again?'"

He doesn't answer for a few seconds that seem to stretch to hell and back.

"What do you mean?" I ask, trying to remember when I ever talked to someone named Damian. I didn't.

"Does the article 'Bodyguards and the City' ring a bell?"

"'Bodyguards and the City?'" I wince. "I... don't know what you mean. Is that some sort of mashup with Sex and the City? Were you in it?"

He shakes his head, pulling out his phone, scrolling, and reading it out loud. "Bodyguards and the City—an article written by... tada... Madison Smith and a bunch of other names."

I wince. "Oh. Was that for the City Paper?"

"Mm-hmm."

"I... I didn't write that article." I clear my throat and straighten my spine. Because he's playing the wrong blame game, and I won't let him drag me down. "I didn't interview anybody for that article. I shouldn't have been on that byline."

"Okay."

He doesn't believe me.

"Oh, and Madison…" His voice drops to one of those husky murmurs that has me wondering when my heart learned how to do these flips. "Thanks for your help in making this interview as great as possible. Maybe we should come up with some sort of schedule? And if I need help, I won't hesitate to ask you. Also, the yoga at the community center for seniors sounds fun. Smiley Face. Smiley Face. Smiley Face."

I frown. I remember those words. Those smiley faces. Me trying to be friendly with the neighbor who had been leaving clothes in the washing machine.

"Listen, I was convinced I was sharing the building with an elderly woman."

The laundry, the books about building muscles in your seventies, the TV volume—it all fit. So, my friendly note was full of Golden Girls-level advice. And now, I find out my neighbor is the human embodiment of a dark romance novel cover? Unfair.

"I do love goat yoga," he whispers next in that growly voice that has my breath getting lost somewhere between my lungs and my lips. A shiver holding a to-do list with only Damian's name on it sprints down my spine, and I clench my thighs together under the table. This man is off-limits, I remind myself sternly. But my body doesn't seem to agree, too busy conjuring up images of Damian's muscular shoulders and torso glistening with sweat, surrounded by adorable goats.

This has me wanting to google the closest goat yoga class.

Ugh.

Relationships aren't for me. Clearly, I can't succeed at them, and humiliation isn't my middle name. If I ever get into a real relationship, I'll know for sure it will be a success.

And a one-night stand with *this* man doesn't spell relationship—it's probably in the dictionary for disaster. No matter how much I wonder how his calloused hands would feel, brushing my spine, digging into my waist, dipping lower and lower. Or how his strong tattooed arms would feel around me, and no matter how impressed I am by his knowledge of Formula One trivia.

I've learned my lesson: keep things professional, focus on my career, and leave the romance to my beloved romcoms and the fictional heroes in my books. Even if they're starting to look a lot like the man sitting across from me.

"So, can we go back to the interview now?"

CHAPTER 6—DAMIAN

Alessandro: Okay, now you look like you're about to bite or laugh.
Aisling: He kind of looks like you there.
Alessandro: Hey. My bites are love bites.
Aisling: Oooookay.

"FINE," I REPLY. "LET'S keep going." Checking the messages on my watch, Alessandro and Aisling seem to be having a blast, watching my reactions. I bring my fingers to my forehead and salute them. They didn't see the headlines, the research Madison Smith has been doing. They don't know this interview isn't really about the school. But about me. Maybe we need to come up with a different plan to spread the word about our classes.

Alessandro: If you answered the questions, maybe it would go faster.

I sigh and refocus on Madison. It's like she's hesitating between digging her heels into the hardwood floor of the bakery and leaping up in the air to flee. Based on the way her jaw is set, it's not solely skipping the interview she's plotting, but skipping town, leaving tire marks behind her like she's racing a Formula One car straight to the podium.

Yet, she stays and lifts her coffee mug up, her fingers trembling slightly. And did I imagine her inhaling against her wrist? That intoxicating scent of hers must be some kind of spell because I would love to do the same.

Sitting even straighter, she sets her coffee mug back on the table—it's one that says, "Coffee first."

"Goat yoga. You love goat yoga." She clears her throat as her eyes focus on the phoenix tattoo on my arm. The one I got after my first tour. I don't even resist the urge to flex—and she raises her eyes back to me. Is that amusement or appreciation in her gaze?

It doesn't matter.

"I do." I lean back in my chair, crossing my arms over my chest. "There's something about those little sounds they make when you're on all fours." And somehow, I managed to make her flush again. I'm tempted to trace the path of her blush and see how far it extends. She was the one who proposed to Chase, the tight end who was everyone's favorite until he started talking about retirement. And, of course, some dumbasses have been blaming her for it. Like they haven't fully understood she was humiliated in front of thousands of people, and I have a feeling Madison Smith doesn't do well with humiliation.

As my mother would say, "There's no shame in falling down. The only shame is in not getting back up."

I wonder if she's read my mom's books. Probably not. She strikes me as the type who focuses on non-fiction and those thrillers featuring journalists. The kind of books where the truth is always black and white, and the heroes always get their day to shine. But life's not like that, and neither are people. We've all got our shades of gray, our secrets, and our scars.

Mine stretch back to a childhood spent bouncing between foster homes, never quite fitting in. I remember how the kids at school mocked me mercilessly when they found out my foster mom was a romance author. They made kissing noises in the hallways, called me her little "research project." As if I was just a means to an end, a prop in someone else's story.

Their words cut deep, deeper than any knife ever could. That night, I grabbed my favorite teddy bear—the tiny one that could fit into my back pocket—and I ran. I ran until my lungs burned and my legs gave out, convinced that my mom was going to send me away, that I was just a temporary fixture in her life.

But she found me. She always did.

I shake my head, shoving those memories back into the steel trap where they belong. No use picking at old scabs. They never heal right, anyway.

Plus, I can't afford to dwell on the past, not when the present is so damn complicated. Madison might not have written that article herself, but she was still involved. Still part of the problem.

"Ok. Great. Goat yoga. Noises. Noted." She taps on the table with her pen, pulling me back to the present.

"I never tried goat yoga before," she murmurs, almost to herself.

Her comment hangs in the air between us, and she glances up at me with an unguarded smile—one that shows a slightly crooked tooth—that has my breath catching. Fine, the woman is cute, adorable, hot. And she knows her Formula One trivia, but she's also calculating. And she didn't say a single word about the article she wrote before. She may not know my name—but Alessandro told her we used to work together. It's like she's buried that moment deep within, hoping I'll forget about it.

But I can't. It's just another reminder of how easily she can twist the truth to suit her needs.

"You lied, you know." My voice isn't a roar. It's not judgment. It's very matter-of-fact.

Her eyes widen slightly. "About what?"

Madison's gaze locks with mine, and for a moment, the bustling bakery seems to fall away. The sunlight streaming through the windows casts a warm glow on her face, highlighting the determined set of her jaw. A distant part of my mind registers the laughter of the other patrons, the scrape of chairs against the hardwood floor, but all I can focus on is the woman in front of me and the defiant tilt of her chin.

"Really? You're going to pretend you don't know. For some reason, I expected better from you."

And it seems I poked right into a gashing wound of her pride because she glares at me. "You expected better? Wow, okay." She inhales deeply. "Making snap judgments is really unattractive, you know."

"I think both you and I know attraction doesn't seem to be a problem."

"I think both you and I know that line is so cliché. And really? You may be ..." She licks her lips, and I'm not sure realizes it. "Attractive. But you know what else is attractive?"

"Honesty. I agree, honesty is very sexy."

"Honesty is sexy. Great. Wonderful. But also, not being a dick..." She glares at me as a chuckle escapes me, and before I can talk about that statement, she cuts me off like she knows she's going to have to agree with what I'm saying next, and she's not up for it.

"Is that really a topic you want to talk about?" I mean to sound aggravated, but my voice has dropped a level at hearing the word "dick" in her mouth. "Because I'm totally up for it." She has no idea how up.

"Oh, I'm sure you are. But this is about the article. If you don't want to do it, just tell me. No need to waste both of our times."

She doesn't need to know I want this article to work. I don't want to let Alessandro or the school down. But this article about me won't be enough. I need her to really see what we're doing, why we're doing it, how we're approaching our school in the community. So, I try a different approach.

"But you need me. Without a willing subject, that portrait is going to be pretty dry," I remind her.

"Listen, I told you I wasn't really involved in that article, and it's true whether you believe me or not," she says, her voice tighter now. "City News had just gotten bought by a company who didn't really respect the AP guidelines. People were leaving left and right. I was a junior staff. That job barely paid the bills since I was just paying my dues and doing research. I get why you're upset. I was upset, too."

Her words are like a match to kindling, igniting the anger I've been trying to tamp down. Upset? She has no idea.

"You think 'upset' covers it?" I snap, leaning forward. "That article nearly destroyed Alessandro's business. It painted us as some kind of shady operation, preying on people's fears. And for what? A byline? A pat on the head from your editor?"

Maddie flinches, but she doesn't back down. "I fought against the angle they wanted to take. I told them it wasn't right. But I was low on the totem pole, and my objections got overruled." She takes a breath, her gaze meeting mine head-on. "I should have pushed harder. I own that. And I'm sorry for the damage it caused." She pauses. "But it's not that article that was really problematic for his business," she points out. "I thought his ex..."

"Yeah, yeah, yeah." I raise my hands because she's not wrong.

"You don't like me." She sounds matter-of-fact like that doesn't bother her, but she's tapping her finger on her thigh. "But you don't have to like me for this article to work."

"Nah, I don't have to. But I have to trust you, right?" I don't even try to growl; it just comes out naturally with her. "So, let's make a deal, Madison."

She winces. "Maddie." It's like she has some sort of Pavlov reaction to hearing her full name. "And what deal are we talking about? Selling my soul to the devil? I think I'll pass. I love the show Lucifer, but I'm not totally sold on selling it to you."

"Selling your soul? Nah, that's not my style. I'm just asking for a little faith, a little trust. Think of it as a down payment on a mutually beneficial partnership." I lift the corner of my mouth. "I need to know you're all in, that's all."

"All in? On what? The article? I'm writing it. That means I'm all in. And if that's the town you're talking about, I didn't know moving to Swans Cove meant forsaking all other plans to move away again." She hesitates as if she didn't expect to blurt that out, while my jaw clenches even harder—soon I'm going to start grinding like I did when I was a teenager, trying very hard not to lose my shit. Because I knew it. She's using Swans Cove the same way she used Alessandro's business. The same way she tried to use her ex.

"You seem highly defensive," I point out.

She inhales deeply—her way, I'm starting to notice, to regain control. And I notice way too much about Madison Smith. "I'm not. This article is about feel-good feelings, bringing something to the community, reminding people that their neighbors have dreams and stories, too."

"Sounds great on paper... but how about this? I'll answer the questions for your profile if you come to one of the Go Seniors and Not-So-Senior's defense classes."

"This wasn't the deal. The deal was you answer questions. I do a portrait filled with warmth..." By the way her pitch goes higher on that last word, it's like she's unsure about that particular aspect.

"Oh, I can give you what you want."

"Again, such a line. And you sound highly full of yourself."

"Nope. Confident." I inch forward, and her sweet floral scent envelops me. It's both mysterious and like a gentle caress, and I have to concentrate on my words and not sniff her like a dog at the shelter. "Just one class." I give her one of those challenging smiles that's part of my arsenal, and I wait for her to say something, but it's like we're on a blink-and-you-lose challenge.

"Wait. I need more." She glances down for a second, taking a few notes. I'm tempted to crane my neck to read her scribbles, but self-respect and years of training have me staying as impassible as possible.

"Oh, I'm sure you do."

She pauses for a moment. But it's like I dared her to do something, and it would appear Maddie doesn't like backing down. Oh no, instead, she lifts her chin and tells me, "Fine. I'll go to one of your Seniors Defense classes if we finish the portrait now, and I'll write another one about the class."

"Fine." I shrug. "You can come to the class next Saturday at 3 pm?"

"Next week?"

"Yep."

She opens her phone and adds it to her calendar. "Great. Now, can we please concentrate on the interview?"

I shrug. "Sure thing." And when she offers her hand for one of those "deals" handshakes, I have the sudden feeling that maybe, just maybe, I'm the one who made a deal with temptation itself.

CHAPTER 7—MADDIE

Rose: My contract got renewed!
Maddie: Congrats!
Mom: We knew it! You're the best!

MY SISTER GOT HER CONTRACT for that new detective show renewed. I'm really happy for her, and yet, I hurry to the next text I received. *Did you see the Not-So-Crabby-News award?* One of my former colleagues sent me with a link to the contest about sharing feel-good stories. It sounds right up my new alley.

I turn on the volume to get in the zone and continue writing the article that's due—I check the clock—very soon. My fingers fly over the keyboard as I listen to my favorite "I'm on a deadline" playlist. For a second, I remember how I never used to play music loudly and sing when Chase was around. It didn't fit the narrative I created for myself, maybe... Or maybe because if he saw all the parts of me, he'd realize they all don't fit...

I shake my head.

Focus on the here and now, Maddie.

Fluffy the Cat, who I adopted last month, jumps on the desk like it's his bed, and I'm clearly interrupting him. He's all soft and sweet, and when I pick him up, my muscles relax, and he cuddles into my arms, doing one of his famous loud Fluffy-purrs. "I'll be all yours in a couple of minutes, promise," I tell him and start typing again.

Hi, Swans Cove, It's Maddie Smith—the new columnist at the Cove Gazette—and I'm thrilled to unveil "Let's Get To Know..." Because you think you may know your neighbors, but are you ready to peel back the layers to reveal the passions that fuel their smiles and drive their spirits? This column is for you who've lived here your entire life or the newbies like me who can't wait to share why Swans Cove has been named one of Maryland's Most Charming Eastern Shore's Small Towns.

Kicking off this series, we spotlight Swans Cove's very own Damian Mack. You may know him from the self-defense school he and Alessandro Torre opened in May. Or you may know him from his volunteering at the shelter where he was nicknamed "The Dog Whisperer," or maybe he impressed you with his trivia skills at Plates & Drinks' Thursday Night Trivia. But are you ready to dig deeper?

I hesitate, considering whether to mention his late-night music jams or maybe drop a line like, "Did you know he has a thing for pink t-shirts?" Or should I touch on his growly voice—the kind romance novels convinced me existed outside of fiction, but I never heard in real life until him? Probably not.

This interview is your golden ticket to seeing a whole new side of Damian, especially with his latest class for seniors and not-so-seniors that I've somehow found myself signing up for.

"Damian... do you know why your parents named you that way?"

I look back up at my computer and pause the recording. That question was one of my last questions to Damian, and I still remember the shadows of pain clouding his eyes. It was only for a few brief seconds, but I found myself wanting to reach out. I didn't. Because the man is a fortress, and I'm a professional. When I mentioned we could skip that one, he insisted he wanted the answer included. If I refused, it would basically be a neon banner of me showing my true colors.

Whatever that means.

I hit play again. "Damian, a demon or an angel? Honestly, I've no idea why my folks went with that name. My biological mom..."

"Biological mom?" I didn't mean to interrupt him, and yet, there's a hint of surprise in my higher-pitched voice. I remember him nodding and making a gesture for me to ask questions. I didn't. Because he was talking. And because I wanted it to be his story. Sometimes coaxing information out of people surprises them in what they end up learning about themselves. Sometimes listening is everything.

Damian's voice fills my small apartment as if he were right there with me, "So, my biological mom had her demons, and my dad... well, he wouldn't have snagged any Father of the Year awards..."

The way he talked about being adopted was almost detached—like this happened to someone else, not to him, but I remember his jaw tensing, his fingers clenching his mug. Like he was daring me to look at him with pity or awe.

I didn't. Because to me, he just looked like the man who'd been keeping me on my toes since he introduced himself. And because he was telling me his story.

He continues, "Definitely not an angel. They were their own Bonnie and Clyde. I was born in jail." A dry laugh breaks through. "Bet that's not the backstory you pegged for me, huh? I don't quite fit the tidy little narrative you had in mind, do I?"

In the recording, my voice doesn't waver. It isn't raw despite the tightening I felt in my chest at his words, because for one split second, I imagined him as a child in the system, and he lost that mask he seemed to have put on: annoyed with me, happy-go-lucky with everyone else, and there was something real there. "Well, first of all, the Devil in the Omen was called Damien—not Damian." I emphasize the "a," and he tilts his head.

"You're a horror movie encyclopedia?"

"I enjoy them."

"Really?"

"I don't quite fit the tidy little narrative you had in mind, do I?" I reply, and he crosses his arms over his chest, watching me. There's something akin to appreciation in his gaze that has me wanting to sit even straighter.

"Maybe you don't."

My voice doesn't tremble as I continue, "Well, Damian actually comes from the Greek name Damianos, which itself comes from the Greek word "damazo," which means to tame or subdue. There's conflicting information about its link to the Goddess of fertility..."

His lips curved into that sexy half-grin then. Sexy and infuriating. Or maybe infuriatingly sexy. "Fertility, huh?"

I can practically feel my cheeks burning, even just from listening back. “So, you’re both a horror movie and a name encyclopedia?” I detect a hint of genuine surprise in his voice, maybe even admiration.

“I may have checked Google when I was trying to make my recorder work and when you went to get a refill on your hot chocolate,” I admit, leaving out the part about how I also ran a case search for possible court records in the state since I finally had his last name—a task Maryland makes surprisingly simple. “I’ll make sure to include that detail if you’d like,” I add.

“Please do. And don’t forget to add that my mom—the woman who adopted me after fostering me for three years and who has been my rock since I was ten—always said my name was mine to shape. And love is about finding someone who helps you be more yourself.” His laughter, dry and knowing, fills the room again. I've written about foster care before. I've witnessed the hard work of dedicated individuals, and I've also seen how the system can sometimes fail everyone involved. Clearly, it failed him for a while. But I'm grateful that this woman fought for him, providing him with a true sense of family. When he calls her "Mom," there's such conviction, fire, and tenderness in his voice that I know she is his mother in every way that matters.

Damian’s got this thing about keeping people safe—maybe that’s what nudged him towards the Navy before he leveled up to a SEAL. Or why he later worked as a bodyguard, dabbled in security, and now teaches everyone in Swans Cove—from kiddos to grandparents—how to defend themselves. His name’s supposed to mean “to tame or subdue.” Growing up shuffled around in foster care, he tried dialing it down, hoping to blend into a family.

But blending in just wasn't in his cards. Instead, he stood out—until he crossed paths with the woman who'd show him that love doesn't mean hiding who you truly are.

That last line has me blinking my eyes rapidly. What the heck?

I inhale deeply and grab my water. That's not bad.

Now let's go more into the other details—and tying it back to Swans Cove.

When asked about what he loves most about Swans Cove, Damian may joke about how it feels like being surrounded by Old Bay (he puts the spice on everything now), but he also talks about how he's enjoyed the people, the town, and the ocean. How he can be by the water with just a five-minute walk through the quaint streets? Or hop on his motorcycle and be by the mountains in less than three hours.

Launching a self-defense and strength mobility class for seniors and not-so-seniors, Damian's proving that it's never too late to pick up new skills and give back to the community. And for a pro tip straight from the man, the myth, the legend himself? "Don't miss out on Aisling's cinnamon rolls... they're nothing short of magical." Can confirm—they're heavenly. Those rolls are going to be my victory treat after I survive Damian's class next Saturday. So, fingers crossed for me.

And remember, always stay true to yourself.

XO,

Maddie.

As I press save, I lean back in my chair, a sense of satisfaction washing over me. Fluffy jumps into my lap, his purrs a gentle rhythm against my legs. I absently stroke his fur as I reread the final lines of the article, a smile tugging at my lips.

This piece is good—really good. It's the kind of writing that could put me back on the map, prove to everyone that Maddie Smith is a force to be reckoned with.

But the moment is short-lived, the memories of the proposal crashing in like an uninvited guest. I feel a familiar tightness in my chest, the echoes of humiliation and self-doubt threatening to drown out my momentary triumph.

After the debacle of the proposal, I'm not sure of my place anymore—not sure of who I am without the accolades, the bylines, the validation of my peers. I inhale deeply, pushing aside the doubts. I have more work to do, more chances to prove myself. I just can't stand in my own way.

The ping of my phone jolts me out of my thoughts. It's a text from my boss, and my pulse quickens as I read the words: "*Crab feast is on Sunday. Perfect for another article.*"

I sit up straighter, my mind already racing with possibilities. I'm sure the crab feast is a major event in Swans Cove—after all, Old Bay is everywhere here. It's a chance to showcase the town's traditions, its sense of community, its heart. And it's a chance for me to prove my worth, to show that I can craft a compelling story that captures the essence of this place and its people.

I glance back up at my trophies and medals: the ones I won for my articles, my High School debate team, my first and only 5k run, my own trivia knowledge. This is my chance to prove I'm still at the top of my game.

Plus, that article could catch the attention of the judges for the Not-So-Crabby-News award.

I've never entered it, but it could be good for me.

A win, and I'll be back on track. I can almost taste the success, the admiration from my peers. I can practically see my byline on the front page, feel the weight of that coveted press pass around my neck, the cheers as I receive my Pulitzer Prize.

I've got this.

Portraits don't work for entering the *Not-So-Crabby-News* competition, but a feel-good piece? Definitely.

But a small, growly, and manly voice sounding a whole lot like Damian murmurs in the back of my mind, "What about Swans Cove? A different life? Maybe a home." I quickly push the thought aside. I can't afford to get attached. And he treats me like he thinks I'm the plague.

Swans Cove is a stepping stone, not a final destination.

If I win the award, it will also be great for the newspaper, the town, everyone. I feel a flicker of excitement, the familiar thrill of a new challenge. One article at a time, one chance to shine. I can do this.

And it's not my way-too-growly-and-grumpy neighbor that's going to derail me from my goals.

But first: shower.

And I guess I should google how to eat crabs.

It can't be that complicated, right?

CHAPTER 8—DAMIAN

Alessandro: How did the rest of the interview go?
Damian: Not terrible.
Alessandro: Well, that's reassuring.

THE SUN IS JUST STARTING to peek over the horizon as Carlos, Noah, and I haul the last of the chairs into place. The air is thick with the promise of heat, the scent of freshly cut grass mingling with the briny tang of the sea. I can feel the sweat beading on my forehead, the rough wood of the chair biting into my palms as I set it down.

"Thanks for the hand, man!" Carlos and Noah call out. We've been at it since the crack of dawn—better to be productive than staying with my damn thoughts anyway.

You might count on one hand the number of Swans Cove residents who won't show up.

"Sure thing," I reply, my voice no longer gravelly with sleep. I hoist one of the prize bags over my shoulder, the canvas cool against my skin. The faint clinking of glass and rustle of tissue paper inside is a reminder of the festivities to come, the laughter and chatter that will soon fill the air. "I'll see you guys at one." The crab feast starts at 3 pm, but I need to be there early. I volunteered to help out, and I'll be manning the dunking booth later, too.

"As long as you don't try to kill us again." Carlos and Noah point to the banner over the table under the oak tree, and I slow down my pace, knowing where their shit-eating grins are heading. "You're not entering one of your, huh, infamous cakes to the baking contest?" Carlos asks, chuckling.

"I make a mean coconut cake."

"Mean wouldn't be the word I'd use," Reed chimes in as he marches toward us with posters in his hands.

"I was trying to be a true Marylander, you know. Smith Island Cake and all..." Who knew that layers could be that hard to assemble? Aisling's been preaching that baking is both art and science, but I still tried to throw a little Damian magic into the mix. I tried to add one more egg and a little less flour because, well, I was running out of flour. Spoiler: it ended in a disaster.

"Maybe..."

"Just make sure to slap a label on it, man." Carlos gives me one of his half-serious looks. "Also, I just wanted to say thanks again for your help with my grandmother. I swear she has been looking forward to that self-defense and strength mobility class of yours."

"She's... worried or?"

"Nope. She's excited for something new." He chuckles. "Plus, she did mention something about seeing you in shorts. Can't say I'm thrilled about her crush..."

I shrug. "I'm here to serve."

And with a wave, I hurry back to my truck, throwing the bag filled with prizes in the back. I've got a few admin tasks to finish, like updating the website, and I have an email from Maddie waiting for me with the subject line: "Last fact check."

Can't wait to see how she twisted and turned my words to make something of a click-bait article.

As I enter the building, I'm greeted by her perfume. Not the essential oil like lavender but her actual perfume. Because there's a difference. She uses lavender for essential oils and roses and vanilla for her perfume. How the fuck is that possible that now I'm going to associate the smell of roses and vanilla with her? And how the fuck did I notice the difference? It lingered here before, and it didn't get me all kinds of bothered, and now, I picture her nails, that tattoo, and that lip color that I really shouldn't want to get all smudged up.

I should take a shower. A polar bear-worthy cold shower. But curiosity takes over, and I plop myself on the stool in my kitchen.

I click on the email from Maddie, my jaw clenching as I scan the biographical details she wrote down. None of the narrative. Just facts. Biographical information, my ass. More like a highlight reel of all the ways she's planning to twist my words and paint me as some kind of charity case.

Like that time a paparazzo yelled across the playground whether I wanted to follow in my parents' footsteps or if I knew about the GoFundMe that had been started for me by a concerned neighbor.

I was eight when my parents abandoned me. I had no fucking clue, and that neighbor was trying to help. She had seen me being taken away from the house kicking, and screaming because I had to leave my cat and dog behind. My mom—when she started fostering me—had that old grumpy cat and my senior dog waiting for me in the house.

When I tried to run away, I always made sure Lightning and Pan were with me.

The tightness in my chest at the memories reminds me of why I never go down memory lane. What's the point?

I can practically see the headlines now: "From Troubled Kid to Small-Town Hero: The Damian Mack Story."

The words blur together, replaced by memories of Alessandro's ex using him for clicks. The article was bad, but she... she could have destroyed him. The clients that vanished overnight, the whispers and sideways glances that followed us for months. And now, Maddie waltzes in with her designer shoes and press pass, ready to stir up trouble all over again.

Something scratches on the floor above me, and then *thump, thump, thump.*

Is she doing jumping jacks in her apartment right now? Or moving furniture around?

I scratch my chin—and reply, "Thanks for that. But I'd like to make sure you're not coming up with some bullshit story. Can you share the headline? Or is your excuse that Ed is coming up with the headline, so if the article is crap, it's not your fault?"

I click "send," wondering if she's going to show up at the crab feast—Ed from the newspaper is always there with a photographer.

Has she even picked a crab before? Why the fuck do I care?

The noise upstairs stops. Maybe she's reading my email. Maybe I should go chat with her in person.

Nope. Not happening. Instead, I head toward the bathroom for that much-needed shower to clear my thoughts.

The water is a shock to my system, but the cold blast doesn't even begin to scrub her image away. I brace my hands against the tile, letting the icy spray numb my skin, hoping it will erase my thoughts. But it's no use. Maddie's image is seared into my mind.

I'm reaching for the soap, my fingers slipping over the slick surface, and her smile floats back to my mind. That and the way her blouse clung to all the right places when she moved. Oh, and the way her eyes flash with challenge and something darker, something that calls to the primal part of me. And it's no longer the early October warm weather that has the heat rising.

I imagine her here with me, her skin slick and warm against mine. I'd back her up against the cold tile, my hands pinning her wrists above her head as I lean in close, my lips brushing the shell of her ear before tracing the rose tattoo with my tongue. "Good girl," I'd growl, feeling her shiver against me, her pulse jumping under my fingers. I'd take my time with her, exploring every inch of her body until she's trembling, until she's begging me for more.

Just when I'm about to take matters into my own hands—literally—to ease the growing ...tension... the water cuts off. I got soap everywhere, and it's no longer tension building, it's frustration. Then the water sputters and dies. The sudden absence of sound is jarring, the silence broken only by the drip, drip, drip of whatever pressure is left in the shower.

The fuck?

I wrap a towel around my waist: a white towel that is now pink after yet another little laundry incident—which makes me think I still have her panties and I should give them back.

As I'm imagining *that* conversation, a drop of water lands squarely on my forehead. What the hell? I look up, incredulous, as another drop follows, the reality of my leaking ceiling setting in. Because my day wasn't FUBAR enough already. Might as well add "amateur plumber" to my resume.

Did she forget to turn off her water? That seems extreme for the water to completely stop, but who knows?

Grabbing her panties, I shove my feet into my beach sandals—the ones that have seen better days—and trek upstairs. My knock on her door isn't exactly what you'd call subtle.

"One second!" She calls out—her voice all muffled and already annoyed. "Ouch!"

The second she opens the door, it's like all the air's been sucked out of the hallway. The blush staining Maddie's cheeks is almost as pink as the towel wrapped around her curves. My fingers twitch at my sides, itching to reach out and touch, to feel if her skin is as soft as it looks.

And with her hair all damp and tousled? Fuck me if that isn't the hottest thing I've ever seen.

I drag my eyes back up to her face, trying to ignore the way my pulse is pounding.

"Matching towels. Guess we've got more in common than we thought, huh?"

She blinks, surprise giving way to a reluctant laugh. The sound shifts something in my chest, makes me want to keep that smile on her face. But then her gaze snags on the scrap of red lace dangling from my fingers, and the laughter dies on her lips.

"Where did you find those?" Her voice is sharp, accusatory. I wince, realizing how bad this must look.

"In the dryer with my stuff. Must have gotten mixed up. Hence why I have a pink towel and pink t-shirts, I remind her." I hold out the underwear, feeling like a kid caught with his hand in the cookie jar despite my annoyance. "I wasn't trying to be a creep, I swear. I just thought you might want them back."

For a moment, it's just us, locked in a stare-down, with the air charged with an electricity that could start a fire, until her eyes start wandering down to my chest. And yeah, I might be putting on a bit of a show, flexing without even thinking. She's taking in the roadmap of scars and burns and tattoos, and when her gaze dips even lower, it hits me: the pink towel is doing a lousy job of concealing how hard I've become.

Her flush descends down to her neck, and I want to trace it with my fingers, my lips, my tongue.

But then her gaze sharpens, as if her brain came up with a thousand theories about what's happening, and none of them are good. "Is that revenge?" Her tone slices through the air between us with a mix of suspicion and accusation. "Did you do that?" Her voice is a spear aimed straight at me, and who needs a Polar Bear Plunge when you have that tone directed at you? That's exactly what Doc ordered to stop the fantasies about Miss Big City Journalist. I can't help but let out a chuckle—not because it's funny, but because of the sheer ridiculousness.

"Do what?" I challenge her to finish her thought.

"Stop the water..." Her hands flail around. "Start a flood. Steal my latest Chewy package," She narrows her eyes. "Is that your way of telling me I'm not welcome in the building, the city, the state?" She pauses. "Shit. Probably the whole universe."

Well, somebody is overreacting.

"Me? Acting like some kind of plumber-mobster criminal?" I shoot back, my words laced with a scoff. Leaning casually against the doorframe, I don't budge an inch, letting the space her suspicion created remain wide open. "Hardly the case," I add, my tone making it clear I'm not about to play into her narrative. "And the package? It's downstairs in the lobby. Maybe you should look down from your pedestal from time to time."

"So not the moment to crack a joke." And is her voice shaking?

I hear a soft meow behind her.

"Close the door!" She sounds panicked, and I do as she says, moving in a protective stance as if a beast is about to attack us. But instead of a beast, she bends down, offering me the best view ever, to pet the ugliest-looking cat I've ever seen. It's clearly old and missing one ear and half of a tail, but its don't-fuck-with-me face that really has me mesmerized. It's the kind of cat who usually stays in a shelter for way too long.

"Hey, Fluffy boy," she whispers in that voice people use with pets. But her tone has me wondering if I'd love my nickname to be Fluffy. Clearly, the lack of zzzz is playing a trick or two on me.

"Fluffy?" I raise an eyebrow, and she glares at me, still petting the cat.

"Yes, Fluffy. He's mine. I adopted him before moving here. Nobody wanted him. He's... mine."

I nod. Because I don't trust my voice.

Maddie now stands up and cradles the cat in her arms, murmuring soft words of comfort, and I feel something—some sort of fissure crack—inside my chest. It's like looking in a mirror and seeing all the broken bits of myself reflected back. The scars, the missing pieces, the fear of never being enough.

Watching Maddie pour her love into this forgotten creature, seeing the way it responds to her touch... damn. That purr's as loud as a Formula One engine revving up. It hits me like a full-force body slam, stirring up a longing I thought I'd buried years ago. Suddenly, I can't breathe, like I'm trapped under a riptide, fighting against a current I never saw coming.

For a split second, I let myself wonder what it'd be like to have someone look at me like that, like I'm worth a damn. Worth holding onto. Worth fighting for. But I slam that door shut fast. Can't afford to go soft—fuck, like my dick's going to let that happen around her anyway. And for what? A woman who's got "trouble" tattooed across her forehead in big, flashing neon. Might as well be carrying a warning label: "Danger: Heartbreak Ahead."

But why, oh, why, does seeing her murmur sweet nothings to this battle-scarred cat in nothing but a towel have me wanting to wrestle the water to make sure she doesn't sound sad ever again?

It's like a glitch in my own personal matrix, where, for a moment, all I care about is her happiness.

But that moment's gone as quick as it came. As soon as the cat jumps down from her arms, she spins back to face me, armor back up, hands on her waist, business mode on full display.

"My ceiling is leaking," she announces, voice tight; all traces of softness vanished like smoke.

"Yeah, well, mine's not exactly dry either."

"You've obviously messed with the laundry somehow."

"Sure, if by 'messing' you mean washing my clothes." I can't help but roll my eyes at City Girl's accusation. Like I've got nothing better to do than sabotage her laundry.

Her gaze narrows, sharp as a knife. "Are you trying to one-up me?"

I shoot back, "Are you, Princess?" The nickname slips out before I can stop it, a jab at her uptight, holier-than-thou attitude. But there's something about the way her eyes flash, the way her cheeks flush with indignation, that makes me want to keep pushing her buttons.

And right now, her entire body tightens.

But then her cat meows again, and she picks him up with such care and love that there's a weird desire in my chest to rush away from this place, this building, this Earth. Maybe Mars is taking applications.

"Toss me your phone, will you?"

She blinks. "What?"

"Your phone. I don't have a phone hidden in my towel. And we got to check in with the building owner, don't we? Do you have his contact saved?"

She nods. "I can contact him myself." Her cat jumps from her arms, and that weird ball inside my throat deflates.

"Go ahead then." I cross my arms over my chest, waiting. And after a few seconds, she lifts her chin back up, and our eyes lock for a heartbeat too long before she clears her throat. "He can't send someone until after the crab feast." She glances around the apartment, then down at her clothes, like she'd never be caught looking like this outside. "I can't wait that long to get ready. I need to be there, too."

Of course, she does. "And I'm supposed to be running a booth there."

She mutters something that sounds a lot like, "Of course you are."

"Let me text Alessandro." And that's when I know she's desperate because she hands over her phone.

"I have his number saved, too," she murmurs, and for a split second, she looks lost, like she's alone in this world. And that tugs something deep inside.

I ignore the feeling and type.

It's Damian—can Madison Smith and I come get ready at your guys' place?

Together? Alessandro writes back, and I imagine him grinning and telling Aisling about his stupid joke.

No. Not together. Our plumbing is having some drama.

Sure thing. Ava woke us up at 5 in the morning, so we're all ready... our showers are yours.

I turn to Maddie. "If you want to get ready, you're welcome to join me at Alessandro's."

She nods. "Thanks."

More time with Madison Smith. Just what I didn't need.

But at least she'll probably be dressed.

CHAPTER 9—MADDIE

Becca: Have you already climbed your downstairs neighbor?
Mads: Nope. Never. Not happening.
Becca: Does he know you dreamed about him?

MORE TIME WITH FORMER Navy Seal, former bodyguard, and current pain in my most-beloved Manolo stilettos.

Just what I don't need.

But I need to finish getting ready. And as I run my fingers through my hair, it's still wet, and some of it clumps together.

Breaking news: There's definitely still shampoo in my hair.

My phone pings again. Damian glances down and back up at me. "Got an email from the Not-So-Crabby News contest," he grunts, and it's my turn to raise an eyebrow at him—annoyance twirling and swirling inside of me.

I lift my chin up, crossing my arms over my chest—channeling my best I can't-believe-you-did-this voice. "How about you don't start reading emails that aren't meant for you? Or is that what you used to do as a bodyguard? Invading privacy?"

His face tightens, and I swear I can see his jaw ticking, ticking, ticking. A part of me is tempted to take cover—my fingers twitching at my sides—but I don't sprint away from problems. My job is to face them head-on. And I frown. His reaction seems over the top for someone who's, yes, annoyed by me but not out of his comfort zone. Banter seems to be his thing.

"Really? You're going there?" he growls in that bear-like voice of his.

I narrow my eyes, counting to three. "I told you I didn't write the article that has your probably very pretty pink panties up in a bunch."

"Probably very pretty pink panties?"

"Uh, I don't know—I liked the alliteration." Plus, my brain seems to let go when it's around him. And I don't know what to do with "letting go." Words continue to rush out of my mouth like there's a fire alarm in there. "And your towel is pink." Why did I just mention his towel? We've established that already. It's pink, and while it covers him, it doesn't hide that this man is an oak tree in all senses of the world. The flush spreading within me like wildfire could have the decency to dry my hair.

But no such luck.

Focus, Maddie. What was the topic? Oh yes, that article.

I tilt my head, definitely not glancing down. "I-I already said I just did part of the fact-checking of that article. I didn't write it. It wasn't, um, a great experience. I've made mistakes in my line of work, but that one wasn't mine. When that was published, I was deep into another assignment." I pause. "I'm sorry the outlet messed up. It's hard enough to open up, but when you do, and it's not taken into account, it sucks." I shrug, my voice unwavering. Because it's true. It's hard enough sometimes to gain people's trust, and that's something I respect. He gives me one of those looks that makes me think that, for once, I am passing one of the tests he doesn't even know he's giving. And as his intense gaze drops to my lips, a shiver carrying his name on a poster jumps up and down my spine.

And I run a hand through my short, drenched hair again.

Once upon a time, I was in control of my image, my heart, my life—now? It's like my body and my mind are racing completely different tracks. And none of them are winning. And my life is well... going along with the mess.

Apparently, my hormones missed the memo that his attractiveness is irrelevant. Even with my barely-passing chemistry grade, I know this reaction between us is just a simple formula.

Nothing more.

Now look away, Maddie. Look. Away. Don't let your gaze travel down his firm torso, trying to decipher what his tattoos mean. Definitely don't continue gazing down to that pink towel again like there's a neon sign pointing to it. Too late. The flush spreading to my neck is spreading... everywhere.

Especially as he steps forward, "And there's no water anywhere else, right?" His voice is deep. Naturally growly? And when his eyes land on the small table by my couch, he frowns. Can he read the highlighted passage in one of my favorite romance novels from there?

Come on, Zoe. Love isn't about being perfect, keeping score, or winning trophies. It's about finding someone who sees your scars and your strengths, your doubts and your dreams. It's supporting each other and growing together—a team without fear of judgment or abandonment. Love is about learning to be more yourself. And you... all the yous: the ones who made you who you are today, the ones you'll be...The very essence of you. I love you. Now, let me worship you with my tongue.

I hurry to close the book, not caring that the shirtless Fabio wannabe on the cover screams "steamy romance" louder than a teakettle. My fingers linger on the well-worn page. How many times have I read this, desperately wanting to believe it? The idea that love isn't about meeting someone's expectations or being the perfect partner is... petrifying, scary, terrifying. Freeing, maybe, but yep, definitely terrifying.

Because if you're not constantly achieving, collecting trophies and confetti, then who are you? Who'll stay by your side? What's left when the applause fades? Been there, done that, got the viral video without the fiancé to show for it. Would give it a 0 on Yelp.

"Lady Grey fan?" He raises an infuriating eyebrow with a half-grin.

It's part "beware" and part "come closer, I dare you,"... which shouldn't make my stomach do some very impressive somersaults. I need water, patience, a portal to a different dimension.

I roll my eyes so hard I'm surprised they don't get stuck, which only makes him clench his hands ever-so-slightly. I'm tempted to do it again just to see what he'd do, ignoring the warmth spreading through my entire body. "She knows how to write earth-shattering orgasms... you know, the kind that only exists in books." And I mean it, she really does.

So, I continue because what was he expecting me to read? Journalism 101? "Not only that... but sometimes, you need fictional book boyfriends. They make you laugh. They make you feel like you matter. And they have the best..." Don't say move. Don't say biceps, Maddie. Don't say— "Tongue. The best tongues."

Did I really just say that to him? To Mr. Muscles-and-Misunderstandings himself?

His eyes darken slightly, but he's also shaking his head like he can't believe this conversation, and heat floods my cheeks.

"You asked," I mutter. "I can read you an excerpt if you'd like some... um, help."

For a moment, something flashes in his eyes that I can't quite read, and his large, calloused hand swipes at his neck. "Woman," he grunts like he's both in pain and... something else.

His falling silent was not what I expected. "Maybe it could be a manual... if you need one."

"Is that a proposition or a book review?" he finally murmurs, leaning in. His scent envelops me, all man and mystery.

Clearing my throat and finding a way to cut the tension with something sharper than a knife, I whirl around. "I need to make sure Fluffy has enough water..." He raises an eyebrow, and I correct myself. "Food. That he has enough food..."

"Fluffy is an interesting name for that cat." He's looking at me with a hint of a confused smile and rubbing the back of his neck like he doesn't realize that makes his muscles flex, and that pink towel moves oh-so-slightly.

Crap. Why am I looking down again? I inch away, focusing on his words—and my desire to show the world that Fluffy is the best cat ever has me snapping out my daydreaming about that very tempting V.

I square my shoulders. "He's definitely a Fluffy." I dare him to say something negative about the sweetest cat in the universe. So what if he looks like a grump and was overlooked at the shelter, and someone once gave him the title of "ugliest cat"? And yes, he can look like he's going to claw your eyes out, but once he knows you? He never would. Plus, once you're in his inner circle, he loves you with everything he has. Large paws, half-tail, and all. And no, not only when he meows at you to carry him to his food like you're his own personal butler.

He chuckles, and the sound has some of the tension melting away like butter on a pan. "I'm surprised you named him that, that's all." And the tension is back. Because, of course, it's not about my cat. It's about me.

"It was the name they gave him at the shelter. I didn't want to change it," I reply, my voice probably telling him he's not marching on eggshells he's barreling into a minefield.

But my answer has him softening—it's in the way there's no longer a challenge in his I-feel-naked-in-front-of-him eyes but an understanding.

More drops resonate into the bathroom, and thousands of scenarios rush through my mind—including one that almost seems reasonable. "Is the water really turned off?"

"I'll check. But I think so—I'm pretty sure there's an issue with the pipes more than the laundry."

"Okay, but what if the water isn't off-off? And then it floods in the apartment?"

"You're worried about Fluffy." At least he doesn't sound surprised.

"I can't really take him with me—he's the sweetest cat, but he has anxiety whenever we go places, and the crab feast is going to be loud..."

"How about this? I'll call Paul again, and I'll make sure the water is turned off. I also have one of those flood devices that will alert me if something goes array."

"So, I could put him in the bedroom—close the door and leave the device on the floor."

"Yep."

Those shivers? They're back full force at him finding solution after solution just to make sure my cat is safe. And now they're singing some sort of symphony, and I can't even sing on key.

"Thank you. I mean it. Thanks." My voice has a soft quality to it, and needing to get back on solid ground, I say, "Let's meet back here in five? Paul seemed pretty responsive." It's not really a question, but I continue, words deciding they have to get out on their own. "If that doesn't work, I won't go. But if it does, I have no idea where Alessandro and Aisling live. Because I'm new...here." I want to clamp a hand over my mouth. What is it about Damian that has me babbling like an idiot? I never do this. I'm the Ice Queen, known for my PRBF and emotional walls, not verbal vomit. Pull it together, Maddie. "Even though getting lost in Swans Cove seems like a feast. It's not very big." Did I just glance down at that stupid, flimsy pink towel? "I mean that... the city is impressive."

Shut up, Maddie. What the heck?

He's leaning against the doorframe now, fully grinning at me. What is it with attractive men leaning against doorframes?

Was there a Masterclass on it? Can I be the reporter who goes undercover to break the story?

And I need to start blinking because those delicious Damian-shivers are getting an upgrade to tingles, and the warning blaring in the back of my mind is the signal I need to get moving.

"So, five minutes," I declare, spinning around before it hits me: I'm in my apartment. He is the one who should be making his exit. And by his low chuckle, he must be thoroughly amused. Forcing myself not to wince and to stay super casual, I whirl back around.

My phone beeps again, and this time, when he glances down, he has the decency to look sorry about it. "Thought it was mine. Your editor wrote." And he hands it over to me. I'm super careful not to even graze his fingers, but of course, I can't ask him to throw it my way like a baseball—plus, I probably wouldn't catch it.

Does he feel the adrenaline, too? Like we're about to speed through Monaco's F1 race's fastest turns: that flat-out kink in the tunnel that can be taken at 160 mph.

Maybe he doesn't. Because he pushes off the doorframe, all casual and smiling. "I'll let you know what Paul says." And then he gives me a strange look—one that has me wondering if he's seeing behind the manicure and the self-confidence. The manicure hides some chipped nails. And the self-confidence? It comes and goes. But at least he doesn't argue and marches back downstairs, and I have two minutes to figure out where I put my self-control and my legendary icy cool demeanor, and off we go.

NEVER MIND ICY COOL.

The email from my editor has me in all sorts of hot-to-the-touch knots. Because apparently, while my article was "all sorts of amazing," I need an additional fun box with questions to make the reader smile.

A fun box to make the reader smile? With Damian? Sure.

At least, it seems that my one-word questions inspired the editor to give me more room in the paper. A full page. Which is amazing, great, definitely encouraging. But now, I need to ask Damian more questions. Which isn't amazing, great and definitely is not encouraging.

"Okay, Fluffy. I'll be back, okay?" I pet Fluffy one more time as I make sure he's secured in my bedroom with food, drink, and access to a litter box. And that flood alarm device's all setup and ready to go. The water is off. And Paul even agreed to have someone come earlier to ensure everything was okay. Fluffy is an inside kitty, and there's no way I'm risking him finding a way out. No way. Not happening. Definitely not. I double-check the door to the bedroom is closed again before hurrying down the stairs.

As soon as I'm outside, I'm relieved to find that the pink towel has been replaced with... faded jeans that hug his muscular thighs. Are you kidding me? And a blue shirt that doesn't hide how well-built Damian is. And is he really that tall? Why am I only realizing that now? Oh, that's right, I'm wearing Converse with a tank top and yoga pants instead of my heels. Something about crab feast makes me think that's more sensible.

He's watching me, and is that appreciation in his gaze? And why do I want to puff like some sort of peacock?

We're standing there for a second too long because I feel the urge to shift on my feet, and like he's pushed by some sort of invisible string, he inches slightly closer to me, and my heart goes on the most terrifying rollercoaster in the world.

"Why the rose?" His voice has that growly tone again, and yet it manages to be warm, too. It's an art, really. His fingers hover over my skin by my neck, and there's that Damian-shiver again. Except this time, it's charged with electricity, and I'm frozen in place.

I clear my throat to make sure it doesn't sound like a crab leg like I've seen on the Plates & Drinks menu got lost in there. "It's pretty," I reply, and that's part of the truth.

"It has thorns."

"Exactly." He chuckles as if he understood exactly what I meant when I'm not even sure why I blurted those words out. There's a story behind that tattoo. A reminder. Just like there's a story behind the tattoo on my wrist and the one on my hip. That one hurt. A lot. And to avoid continuing to blurt stories I don't mean to tell, I finally step away from him. Is it now easier to breathe or harder?

I shake my head as his infuriating half-grin is firmly back in place. "Let's go." I start walking. "We don't want to be late."

"Then, you might want to go that way," he tells me with a deep chuckle, and I whirl around, falling into step next to him without another word.

And as we hurry through Swans Cove, my eyes keep on glancing toward the storefronts—the happy fonts and the punny names. "Once Upon A Brie," "Meow Books." The fall décor has started with posters of the "Howl-oween" parade.

"Is that an annual thing?" I ask, pointing toward the pumpkin with a dog inside of it.

He nods. "A big fundraiser for the shelter. That and the Pet with Santa pictures are a hit."

As we walk side by side, I can't help but steal glances at Damian from the corner of my eye. He's undeniably gorgeous, all rugged and rippling muscle, but it's more than just his physical appearance that draws me in. It's the way he interacts with the people we pass, the genuine warmth in his smile when he talks about his volunteer work at the animal shelter.

There's a softer side to him, one that's at odds with the tough, guarded exterior he presents to the world. A side that makes me wonder about the scars he carries, both visible and invisible.

I quickly look away before he can catch me staring, my heart doing a traitorous little flip in my chest. I can't afford to get distracted by a rugged Thor lookalike with more tattoos and scars and a mysterious past. I'm here to do a job, to prove myself as a reporter. Falling for my prickly, too-hot-for-his-own-good neighbor is definitely not part of the plan.

Older gentlemen playing Scrabble at a terrace ask him whether or not he's going to come play piano at Plates again.

He gives them their full attention—it's only a few seconds, but it's there. It seems genuine. Real.

"You play piano?" I ask as we continue walking.

"Yep."

"That didn't come up during the interview."

"Nope."

I half-expected to carry on a conversation, but I clearly should know better.

I continue, "You really like it here," I tell him. After all, I have to finish that interview. Talking might be necessary.

He cocks an infuriating eyebrow again. "And you're clearly Sherlock Holmes."

"I watch a lot of slashers and thrillers... For some reason, I always know who the bad guy is."

"And you think I'm the bad guy?"

Is my heart stuttering? Yep. Definitely a bad guy. The type that could get me to open up to better slash my emotions into shreds.

Been there. Done that.

"Nope. Not what I said." And then I wince. "Also, while we're chatting like totally normal people, can I ask you a few more questions? Ed—from the newspaper—asked me to expand the article. So, I came up with a few "this or that" that could make it fun."

He nods reluctantly. "Sure. Fine."

That's the spirit.

CHAPTER 10—DAMIAN

Voicemail: Hi lovey, it's Mom. I'm thinking about coming today. I'm not sure you can hear me... I'm trying those new earpods I got and beeeeeeeeeeeep. *Do you listen to your voicemails?* Beeeeeeeeeeeep. *I love you.*

"I'LL ASK YOU ABOUT ten this or that questions and keep five," she says. Her voice is throaty, like a podcaster's, capturing my attention.

Then, that scent of hers hits me. It's like a stealth attack, bypassing all my defenses and heading straight for my brain. And, uh, other regions. Which is all kinds of wrong, considering she was just gushing over my mom's steamy novels.

I can't help but smirk. It's funny, in a twisted sort of way. Here I am, getting hot and bothered by a woman who probably thinks my mom's fictional heroes are the pinnacle of manhood.

If she only knew...

"What's your perfume?" I don't blurt the question out. Oh no, as we stop to let Mr. Blackwell and his kids go by, I lean slightly forward, giving her my full attention. Her eyes flash to mine, narrowing like no one has ever asked questions about her.

“My perfume?” She repeats, staring straight ahead as we continue strolling around town toward Aisling and Alessandro’s house.

“Yep.”

“You do know I’m the one writing the article, right?”

“We’re clear on that.”

The silence that stretches between us is almost as heavy as the humidity that seems to rise from the pavement.

After a few more seconds, she declares, “Sí by Georgio Armani.” And then continues, like this was some sort of negotiation I wasn’t aware of. “The Crown or Bridgerton?” she inquires, prompting an involuntary raise of my eyebrow as if it’s hard-wired to react to her questions. And I didn’t see that one coming.

“The Crown for you, isn’t it?” I reply, and she shakes her head.

“The questions are for you, not for me. But just so you know, I actually watch both.”

“Oh, really? Favorite quote of Bridgerton, then?”

She comes to an unplanned stop and that’s when I know I’ve gotten under her skin as she mutters something to herself. Without make-up, I can see a few freckles on the bridge of her nose. They really shouldn’t be that fascinating. And yet, I want to count them, ask her if she’s always had them, see what kind of shape they make.

I continue, my voice huskier. “Mine is from season two: ‘You are the bane of my existence—and the object of all of my desires.’” I deliver the line dramatically, and I’m rewarded with a genuine smile. One that shows on her face, her eyes. Her entire body seems to relax for a split second.

But too quickly, she must realize she let down her guard and clears her throat. "Great. I'll add that to the "Get To Know Damian" Box." She starts walking again, in the wrong direction, when my arms find the crook of her elbow—and are we both feeling that spark of electricity, or is it something in the air?

"You're going the wrong way," I tell her, and she follows me without a word at first.

After a few seconds, she licks her lips like she's trying to regain some sort of control. "It's really warm here in October..." She grabs her recorder from her purse. "I fixed it," she mutters, like talking about her recorder grounds her in the moment, "It needed batteries."

She readjusts the small sports bag she's carrying, probably with what she needs to get ready. But that bag has my eyes widening and a grin spreading on my lips. Because that bag doesn't scream Miss Proper and Put-Together Madison Smith.

"Are those movies' serial killers?" I gesture towards the eclectic drawing, recognizing figures like Ghostface from *Scream*, Jason, Michael Myers, and others crammed into a car.

She confirms with a simple "Yep." And am I smiling at the fact she's using my one-word answer?

"Here, let me help you," I offer, but her grip on her bag tightens.

"I've got it," she replies.

"Okay..." I take another look at the bag. "Was it a prank gift or something...?"

The sound that escapes her lips is a mix of frustration and amusement, and I can't help but imagine what other sounds I could coax from her. I wonder how she would react if I pulled her close, my hands gripping her hips as I backed her up against a wall. Would she gasp in surprise, her eyes darkening with desire? Or would she meet me halfway, her lips crashing against mine in a fierce battle for dominance?

The thought has heat reeving its very loud engine through my body, and I have to clench my jaw to not ask her if she feels it too. My hands curl into fists, and it shouldn't be that hard to stop wanting to reach out and touch her. It's a visceral reaction, one that catches me off guard with its intensity. I've never wanted someone so badly, so quickly.

It's like Maddie has awakened a thirst in me that only she can quench. As if I've been turned into a vampire, and she's the only one I crave. Apparently, falling asleep to Twilight wasn't my best idea ever.

It must be the hot weather; it's messing up some of my brain's connections.

Her throaty voice snaps me out of my thoughts. "My sister gave it to me for Christmas."

"As a joke?" I grunt, trying to piece together her apparent interest.

"Nope," she clarifies. "As I mentioned, I really enjoy scary movies." Her tone is clipped, and she continues without another beat. "Pancakes or Waffles?"

"Waffles," I declare, letting a smile creep across my face—one that I know has a history of either getting me out of or directly into trouble. As we're about to enter Alessandro and Aisling's home, I add, with a growly tone that seems to become more frequent around her, "But back to Bridgerton, I'd love to know your favorite quote?"

Her gaze drops to my lips, a tempting flush spreading on her neck. And forget the reeving engine, it's like a fucking inferno erupts in my veins. The desire that slams into me is so raw, so primal, that it takes my breath away. I'm instantly hard, my cock straining against the confines of my jeans, demanding attention.

I watch as she drags her tongue along her bottom lip, the action so sensual that I can't suppress the low growl that rumbles in my chest. I want to grab her, to haul her against me until every inch of her is pressed against my hardness. I want to devour her, to taste every single part of her until she's writhing in ecstasy.

The fantasies that flash through my mind are so vivid that I'm surprised the air doesn't combust between us. I imagine bending her over the nearest surface, tugging down those yoga pants that hug her ass, and burying myself deep inside her tight heat. I picture her on her knees, those pouty lips wrapped around my cock as she looks up at me with those big, definitely not innocent eyes.

"From the show?" Her voice brings me back to the here, and now and I have to remind myself what we're talking about. "I have two." She must see my somewhat confused face because she tilts her head. "From Bridgerton. The first one is, 'I know some men cannot perform without their familiar tools. Like a child with a blanket.'"

And the laughter that escapes me is deep, genuine, loud.

Real.

Her lips curve into a smile at the sound—and I want to take a picture. To keep that smile in my back pocket for shitty days full of shadows.

"My tool is very important, that's true." My tone is teasing. I'm tempted to tell her I know how to use it… but instead, I want to know more about her. About what makes her tick. And those questions reveal some things I didn't expect. "What's your second favorite quote?"

Her fingers play with her necklace—a heart-shaped silver necklace, and I want to ask her about that. I want to ask her about everything.

"'We are not all guaranteed a fairy-tale ending.'" Her eyes find mine, and in hers, there's almost a dare as if to challenge me to contradict her.

"For once, we agree on something," I reply with a shrug. "And you know what? Not everyone wants a fairy-tale ending." I don't tell her no one deserves my brand of bullshit. After all, we all have scars that are hidden so deep we hope no one sees them. Ever.

The door swings open as a shadow of understanding passes between Madison Smith and me. It's a fleeting moment, but it feels significant like we've just stumbled upon a shared truth we both recognize but rarely acknowledge.

"Uncle Damiaaaaaaaaaaaaaaaaaaaan!" Ava sprints toward us, and I hurry to catch her before she even steps on the sidewalk. Ava giggles—the sound carefree and happy—and every nerve in my being wants to make sure this little girl only has moments that make her smile. She hangs on to me like I'm a playground and loudly exclaims, "Hi, Princess Maddie."

In her voice, Princess sounds like a term of endearment, but as I turn around and whisper, "Princess Maddie," said-princess' smile turns into a frown that stings more than I'd like to admit.

"Don't," she whispers, her voice tight with an emotion I can't quite decipher. It's the same reaction she had earlier when I called her Princess, and I realize I've inadvertently hit a nerve. There's a story there, a wound I've accidentally prodded, and while I may not know the details, I understand the impulse to keep certain parts of yourself locked away.

I meet her gaze, holding it for a moment as if to say, "I get it," before turning my attention back to the little girl who holds my heart in her hands.

As Ava chatters on about her drawing with Maddie, I find myself studying my neighbor from the corner of my eye. She's smiling at Ava, but there's a wistfulness to her expression that makes me wonder if she's thinking about her own childhood, her own family. It's a shade of vulnerability I haven't seen from her before, and it only makes me want to know more.

"So, how long is your contract with the Gazette?" I ask during a pause where Ava is now pretending to snore like her dog, trying to keep my tone casual. Not sound accusatory. There, a normal conversation. "Are you planning on sticking around Swans Cove for a while, or is this just a temporary stop?"

Maddie's gaze snaps to mine, surprise flickering in her eyes before she quickly shutters it. "I thought you already made up your mind that I was just, you know," she mouths the word "using people." And because Ava is no longer playing "snore" and is paying attention to our conversation, she continues, "I'm not sure yet," she says, her voice carefully neutral. "I guess it depends on how things go here, what kind of stories I find."

"Oh, you need to stay," Ava says, and then she starts singing a song she probably made up herself. And hearing the little girl's sad voice, I wish I could protect her from heartache.

Madison bites her lip. "You know, what if we're friends? Sometimes distance doesn't matter. I don't see my sister all the time and I love her just the same." She pauses. "I do miss her, though. So, I get it."

Ava nods and changes her song to "All I want is another dog." I'm guessing she's been making up songs about wanting more pets.

On one hand, the thought of Madison leaving shouldn't bother me. I don't do commitments, and I sure as hell don't need the complication of getting involved with someone who's going to be sticking around. It's better for both of us if she's just passing through.

But on the other hand, the idea of her walking away, of never getting to explore this crackling tension between us, leaves a bitter taste in my mouth. If she's not planning on staying, then what's the harm in seeing where this thing could go? It's not like I'd be breaking my rules if there's no chance of it turning into something serious.

CHAPTER 11—MADDIE

Rose: Hey, Mads, just checking in... You won't believe who I saw on set! Grant Torre!!! His brother lives in Swans Cove, right? Work is good. How is Swans Cove? And um, how is that neighbor of yours?

MAYDAY. MAYDAY.

The alarm blaring in my mind needs to be silenced. I take a deep breath, focusing on the steady rhythm of my pulse. Losing my composure here, now, on a street lined with magazine-cover-worthy houses, isn't an option—especially not with Mr. Hot and Sexy Former Bodyguard gazing at me with those intense, understanding eyes.

As if he sees right through my icy attitude.

But he doesn't.

He can't.

I won't let him.

I square my shoulders and flash a confident smile, refusing to let the panic take over.

"Mom and Alessandro have been reading fairytales to me," Ava's words tumble out like she's in a hurry to tell the story.

Her chatter about princesses brings a smile to my face, but the nickname "Princess Maddie" feels like a weight on my chest, dragging me back to memories I'd rather forget.

The title of "Princess" has never been a crown for me—it's been a curse. From the kids at school mocking me as the "Ice Princess" when I refused to cry, to my sister throwing those words at me during an argument, to my first boyfriend spreading rumors about my apparently legendary frigidity, those words have always been a weapon wielded against me.

I feel that old familiar panic rising in my chest, but I force myself to breathe deeply. I remind myself that I've faced tougher situations before. Running or hiding isn't an option. I square my shoulders and focus on the present moment, on the scent of cinnamon wafting by, refusing to let fear take control—even if part of me knows that I'm hiding part of myself. Always shoving the most vulnerable parts down and away from people.

From myself.

I inch away from Damian, needing space to breathe, but my body betrays me. My skin prickles with awareness, every nerve ending attuned to his presence. When he turns to face me, his gaze intense and questioning, I suppress a shiver, heat coursing through me like an electrical current.

I must be lacking major sleep. That's the only explanation for those butterflies taking a bubble bath in my chest.

Ava chirps again, "Sometimes, in fairytales, it's insta-something." She climbs further on Damian as if he's playground equipment and switches topic when she notices the phone in my hand. "Mommy doesn't want me to have a phone yet. Daddy agrees. Alessandro, too," she declares. Then she adds, "And those princesses? Well, they didn't have phones either. But you have a phone, and you look like a princess who can do everything! That's why you're Princess Maddie."

Damian's deep chuckle doesn't hide the slight concern in his frown as he's still looking at me. I inch away, needing my breathing to stop taking detours. But the air is still oppressive with humidity.

I want to blurt out everything to him. Which makes no sense. When I tried therapy, I didn't share those moments, those feelings. Because losing it in front of the person who was there to help me felt wrong. I failed at therapy. And maybe that's why I never went back.

And why am I thinking about therapy now?

Ava whispers something in Damian's ear, and he nods. "Well, you have to ask her, though."

Ava's shy smile has me smiling back at her despite the turmoil still roiling through my chest.

"I'm going to the crab feast, too. Can you sit with us, please? Pretty please?"

Alessandro chooses this moment to step out. "I told Ava she could lead you inside, but I've been watching from the window, and it seems she's got quite a few stories to tell." His voice is warm, and Ava manages to jump off Damian's arm to rush back to her stepfather.

"I asked Princess Maddie to sit with us at the crab feast. She can, right? Please."

Alessandro gives his full attention to the little girl, like she's the most important person. Both he and Damian have this magnetic presence. Maybe it's the height or broad shoulders or the tattoos... or maybe it's just the way they carry themselves.

But while Damian has more of a casual this-is-who-I-am-and-I-can-be-fun commanding presence, there's nothing nonchalant about Alessandro, and yet he seems to be turning into pudding with the little girl.

"You need to ask her and make sure it's okay with her. And if it is..." He doesn't finish his sentence. Instead, he gives me a look that tells me he's studying me, my reactions, maybe even analyzing me like he used to do as a bodyguard, bracing for potential dangers, and it's impossible to relax under that stare. Instead, I tense up, remembering that article that was published on his business and whether he thinks I was responsible for it. I shouldn't care. But little Ava has me wanting to pass that test I didn't sign up for.

Damian clears his throat and steps in front of me as if he's shielding me from that stare. Annoyance flares deep within. I'm no princess—definitely not one in distress. I can protect myself. I can stand on my own. I don't need him to do whatever former SEAL, bodyguard, Damian-thing he's doing. But what really annoys me? It's that even though I bristle at the idea of needing protection, a tiny part of me feels a flicker of relief, of longing. What would it be like, just for once, to let someone else carry the burden? To let myself be vulnerable?

Nope. Not going there.

Damian's head shifts slightly as if he's attuned to my reactions, and Alessandro finally finishes his sentence like they had some sort of silent conversation no one else was privy to, "And if it is, it's okay with us—I'm sure your mom will say yes, too."

Us.

He and Aisling are a team.

They know each other. She trusts him. I can see it in the way he said that last sentence.

When Damian turns to me, and I glance up and up at him, his eyes narrow slightly.

"You okay?" He asks again. There's an undertone of concern in his gruff voice. A gruff voice that seems to bury itself deep under my skin, awakening nerves I didn't even know existed. And that grates me.

I force myself not to shift on my feet. The alarm blaring in my mind has turned into a silence that's even more unsettling.

I'm tempted to say no, turn around, forget the whole thing. Maybe I need a bath. Oh yes, that's right, my apartment is flooded. And I need this article to prove myself.

Plus, Ava's looking at me like her entire day hangs on my answer. I don't want to disappoint her.

"Yep. Great." I manage a everything-is-cool tone that has me pretty proud of myself. "Sitting together will be perfect so I can finish asking you questions." I tap my back pocket with the recorder because that's what I need to remind myself: this is all for work, for me to find a place in Swans Cove. "You do sit down at some point, right?"

His gaze doesn't leave mine and why, oh, why do I feel even more unsettled than when Alessandro was clearly assessing me? Maybe because when Damian looks at me, there's this crackling tension in the air, and I'm not sure if it's going to lead to fireworks... or an explosion.

Definitely a distraction.

And I can't afford distractions, not when I'm so close to regaining everything I've ever wanted—respect, success, a chance to make my mark.

Damian Mack might be temptation on a very thick stick, but he's a complication I don't need. I'll get my story, make nice with the locals, and keep my eye on the prize.

No matter how tempting he might be.

CHAPTER 12—DAMIAN

Carlos: We're going to be setting up the dunking booth first. See you then. Also, Reed was asking about your neighbor. Is she single?

I SHOULD HAVE BEEN here earlier, helping to set up for the crab feast instead of playing tour guide to Madison Smith. But as soon as we entered the park and all eyes turned towards us, I knew I had to put some distance between us. The last thing I need is the gossip mill churning out dating rumors.

"Thanks again, man," Carlos says as he hauls over a stack of heavy paper rolls for the tables. The cleanup is going to be a nightmare. But hey, if it keeps our firefighters equipped, I'll scrape Old Bay off tables till my fingers bleed.

One of the fire trucks needs repairs, and the money raised from today's feast will go a long way. Landon Adams, Aunt Locelli's nephew, has already done a lot for the station—renovations, new equipment, making sure the firefighters are taken care of. But every little bit helps.

I nod in response, my focus on checking the grill setup for the corn on the cob and burgers. The scent of charcoal and lighter fluid fills my nostrils, familiar and comforting. This is what I need; the simplicity of manual labor, not the complicated mess of feelings that Maddie stirs up in me.

As I work, I can't help but overhear the excited chatter around me. There's the dessert contest, of course, sponsored by Aisling and Alessandro. The winner gets their choice of a baking class at the bakery or a self-defense session at our school. I make a mental note to add some postcards promoting our upcoming senior and not-so-seniors' class to the prize bowl, cursing myself for forgetting to grab them earlier. My mind was a little preoccupied with Maddie's leaking ceiling, and the way her skin flushed pink, and the way her heart seemed to shine through her eyes when talking about that ugly cat.

I force my thoughts back to the present, scanning the program for the other events. The shelter's "Name a Pet" contest has my jaw clenching—I want this to work. I want to bring attention to some of the pups who've been waiting a long time for their forever homes, like my buddy Barkey, who's been at the shelter for months now. He's a great dog, loyal and loving, but he's been overlooked time and again. Older. A throaty bark that he can't seem to control. There are a dozen dogs and cats and more like him. I know that look in their eyes. Seen it in the mirror enough times. That "please don't send me back" look. It's a look I gave to foster parents who were trying their best—and to my case worker, who knew the system was failing me. It hits harder than a flash-bang in close quarters every damn time.

I'm halfway to the grill, lost in thought, when a burst of laughter snaps me back to reality.

It's a carefree sound. Happy. Warm. Throaty. And it wraps around my chest like a comforting hug.

I look up to see Maddie surrounded by a group of firefighters, Reed front and center. He's leaning in close, hanging on her every word like she's the most fascinating thing he's ever seen. Something hot and prickly claws at my insides, my jaw clenching tight.

Reed's a good guy—the kind who's looking for a real connection, someone to build a life with. He doesn't deserve to get burned by a woman who's just breezing through town—even if she has a laugh I want to bottle and listen to at night when I wake from a nightmare.

Before I can think better of it, I'm striding towards them, my feet moving of their own accord. It's like there's a magnetic pull drawing me to Maddie, some inexplicable force that won't let me stay away. I don't know what I'm going to do when I reach her—drag her away from Reed? Pull her into my arms and show everyone that she's mine? It's ridiculous, possessive, completely out of character for me. But when it comes to Maddie, all my careful control seems to evaporate.

I'm just a few feet away when a familiar voice stops me dead in my tracks.

"Ohhh, ohhh, honey!"

I freeze, my eyes slamming shut. Mom. Love you, but your timing's for shit. And now I'm going to have to play twenty questions about my love life. Fan-fucking-tastic.

I can feel Maddie's curious gaze on me from across the grass, and then her eyes widen. Did she recognize my mother? She had her books, after all. Highlighted and everything.

And I know, with a sinking certainty, that my mother's presence here is only going to complicate things even further.

As if things between Maddie and me weren't messy enough already.

CHAPTER 13—MADDIE

Order notification: Your pre-orders of The Wallflower's Duke and Puck of Revenge have been delivered.

OHMYGOD. OHMYGOD. OHMYGOD.

I pride myself on always being in control, but seeing *the* Lady Grey standing just a few feet away has my heart doing somersaults.

How does she know him?

My brain goes through everything I know about Lady Grey. Does she have kids? She has a son. But his name is Adam. Not Damian.

Right?

But Adam was adopted, too. Oh my, is Damian her son?

I have her latest novels tucked in my bag, the pages worn from countless re-reads. And they both came out last week. She releases two books a year—one in her regency romance world and the other in a dark-ish hockey romance. Both worlds have spice and love and gives all the flutters. He's seen the cover of my favorite one. Probably noticed the highlighted parts. I told him about... the moves of the amazing and panty-dropping book boyfriends his maybe-very-probably mother writes about.

Ugh.

Despite the heat creeping up my neck, it takes every ounce of willpower not to rush to her to ask for her autograph or beg for details about a potential sequel to *My Favorite Viscount*.

I want to inch closer, but I restrain myself for a few more minutes, giving them privacy, until Ava waves my way.

When I approach, Damian's back is turned to me, and he's clearly incensed about something. His sharp words to Alessandro slice through the air.

"I swear, the next thing that's going to happen is the Ice Princess over there asking for an interview. She's not using my mother for fodder. That's for sure."

"The Ice Princess?" Alessandro asks, and Damian's answer is lost in the buzzing of my mind... how did he know that nickname? Is there a reel I missed? A highlight of my most humiliating moments?

I feel the blood drain from my face, my heart stuttering to a stop before kicking into overdrive.

Damian grunts, "I don't know, man." He rubs the back of his neck. "Your daughter was talking about princesses. Singing Frozen. If the fairytale fits..."

The title I've tried so hard to shed, the armor I've worn for so long that it's become a second skin. Hearing it from Damian's lips, in that harsh tone, is like being stripped bare in front of the whole town.

I swallow hard. I won't let him see how much he's hurt me, won't give him the satisfaction of watching me crumble.

Because I don't crumble.

Lady Grey steps closer to them. "The Ice Princess, you said? Who is that?" Lady Grey's voice is calmer than her son's. Her son. So, I did gush about the way she writes scream-from-pleasure orgasms to her son. That's great. Plus, I definitely want my favorite author to know me as the ice princess.

I square my shoulders and march right up to Lady Grey, my hand outstretched and a brittle smile plastered on my face.

"Hi, Lady Grey. I'm a huge fan." My voice is steady, betraying none of the turmoil raging inside me. "I'm... Madison Smith... the Ice Princess."

I stare right at Damian when I say that, and his gaze bores into me, his presence as tangible as the heat of the October sun on my skin.

Lady Grey's eyes widen in surprise, darting between her son and me. But to her credit, she takes my hand without hesitation, her grip warm and firm.

"It's lovely to meet you, dear. I know you met my son. He's got a sharp tongue sometimes, but he's all marshmallow inside."

Tongue. A sharp tongue. Oh. My. I told him about the way *his* mother writes the best book boyfriends, with the best tongues. Don't start giggling, Maddie. You're a reporter, a professional. You can do this.

"I did," I croak out. Because, yep, I definitely met her son. "I... I thought your son's name... Adam?" And I can no longer form sentences. Great.

She tilts her head, her voice soft. "Adam is actually his middle name. I always want to protect his privacy." She gives me a smile. "I've heard so much about you from Alessandro and Aisling. All good things, I assure you."

I take a deep breath, willing my cheeks not to flush. "It's an honor to meet you, Lady Grey. Your books are..." Amazing? Inspirational? A masterclass in romantic tension? "...They've been a bright spot during some tough times."

There. Honest without being embarrassing. But now Lady Grey is smiling at me like she knows exactly which scenes I've dog-eared, and I'm fighting the urge to ask her to sign my well-worn copy of *My Favorite Viscount.*

Come on, Maddie. You've interviewed athletes and local leaders without breaking a sweat. You can handle your favorite romance author. Just don't mention tongues again. Or marshmallows. Or anything, really. Maybe I should just smile and nod for the rest of this conversation?

"I'm glad that I've brought sunshine to your life. That really makes me happy."

Her words soothe some of the sting of Damian's earlier barb, but as I glance around, I notice the crowd gathering. People are chatting, laughing, sharing inside jokes about town events I'll probably never get invited to—unless it's with my press badge. My smile slips into place automatically – the same one I've worn at countless networking events and interviews.

But for once, I don't want to network. I don't want to find the perfect quote or angle for a story. I want to ask Lady Grey about her characters, about how she crafts those heart-wrenching scenes and those giggle-out-loud moments that kept me company on lonely nights. I want to just... enjoy this moment.

Instead, I'm standing here, nodding along, my notepad untouched in my bag. Always the observer, never quite part of the story. Is this what it feels like to be a side character in someone else's novel?

I shake off the thought. I'm Maddie Smith, award-winning reporter, master of the angle, of the question, of digging deeper. I don't do starstruck.

I can't.

Because all those stars in your eyes don't win prizes or respect or ...I shake my head.

Maybe it's time to embrace the Ice Princess, to wear her like a badge of honor instead of like a scarlet letter.

Maybe that's what a winner would do. But why does it suddenly feel like I'm playing the wrong game?

CHAPTER 14—DAMIAN

Paul: The plumbing is having more issues than we thought... I'd ask my favorite Walking Grandma, but she's at the crab feast. Will keep you and Madison Smith updated. Have fun!

SHIT. FUCK. SHIT. FUCK.

"Hey," I start—not mumbling because this isn't the moment to mumble or even growl. The only reason I said the "Ice Princess" was because I was a) worried about my mother being here, and (b) Ava had just sung *Let It Go,* and I was stuck on it. Not my best moment. Especially because, despite her smile, I can see the hurt behind Madison's straight spine. It's in the way she grips her purse with one hand and the shadows in her eyes.

Madison tilts her head, ignoring me. "Well, I'm glad someone had good things to say about me."

I wince, shadows of guilt twisting in my gut. I want to explain, to apologize, but the words stick in my throat.

"I've been a fan of yours ever since my mom read your first novels..." Maddie says to my mother, her voice filled with admiration.

"Your mother?" My mom laughs. "I'm so glad I can bring people together."

Maddie's smile falters slightly, and I catch the flash of hurt in her eyes. I feel a sudden urge to reach out, to comfort her somehow, but I hold back.

"Also, if you'd like to chat with me about an article, don't hesitate," my mother continues. "I appreciate the work you've been doing."

Maddie's eyes widen, surprise and, is that gratitude in her expression? "You mean journalism?"

"Yes." My mother nods. "But I'm talking about you. I read that article you wrote about the oncology nurses who make their world a brighter place."

I uncross my arms, watching the exchange. I've been so focused on my own reservations about Maddie's work that I never stopped to consider the impact she's had. Hearing my mother's praise shifts something in me, a subtle realignment of perspective.

Maddie ducks her head as if hearing compliments wasn't something she was used to. "Thank you. It really means a lot. I haven't done any investigative pieces in a while. I also love sharing local stories. And that's one of the reasons I'm here. You know, there's so much joy to share, too. And uplifting moments. It's all about finding a balance." She pauses, her voice turning rueful. "Plus, I got fired from my last two jobs. Granted, the first one was because the outlet got bought by one of those big conglomerates, and I didn't want to toe their line." She lifts her chin as if reliving that conversation. "The second was... well... I messed up—my articles weren't as good. I thought using my personal life would help, and it backfired."

My heart clenches at the vulnerability in her admission. I know a thing or two about losing your way, about feeling like the fire inside you has burned out. My fists tighten at my sides, an echo of the frustration and despair I've felt in my own lowest moments.

"Oh, honey, I know," my mother says softly. "I've been waiting to write a sequel to *My Favorite Viscount*." Maddie's mouth gapes open before a grin spreads on her face. She's a fan. A true fan. My mom continues, "But... I've been wondering about them. About what makes them fight for one another. And I know people want more of them. I give Happily-Ever-Afters, and this one ended on some sort of Happy-For-Now. I feel like they're guarding the broken shards of their heart so tightly hidden that they can't even share them with one another yet..." My mother sighs. "Listen to me going on and on and on about my job."

"I love your work," Maddie tells her. "Getting lost in one of your stories? It's really like a warm blanket on a cold night."

"With spiced wine? It gets spicy in there."

I groan. Because it's like they both forgot I was standing right here.

Maddie's brow furrows. "How did you find that article about the hospital?"

My mother chuckles. "Oh, honey, I know how to Google."

The statement startles a laugh out of me, breaking the tension that had settled over the conversation. Leave it to my mom to do her research and catch us all off guard.

As the two women continue to chat, I find myself watching Maddie, seeing her in a new light. She's a fighter, someone who's been knocked down but keeps getting back up. Just like me.

And maybe, just maybe, we're not as different as I thought.

Especially as Maddie clears her throat and says, "You know what? I've been thinking about entering the crab-eating contest. Give my article more of a flair, you know."

My mom claps her hands together like this might be the inspiration for her next romance novel. But I can't help but let out one of those low chuckles that tell more stories than sixty thousand words.

"What?" Maddie crosses her arms over her chest.

"Well, you're not going to win," I state, the words coming out more matter-of-fact than I intended. "You have to eat three crabs the fastest way possible. Have you even ever picked a crab before?"

"I know how to YouTube things." The way she says that has my mom's gaze dancing from Maddie to me with a smile I know all too well. That's her Lady Grey smile. The one she uses with readers when she says, "I smell love in the air." No, Mom. What you smell is Old Bay, not love.

I gesture for Maddie to step away while Ava takes my mother by the hand to show her her newest drawing: dogs playing together.

"You're sure about this?"

"Definitely." Maddie's nostrils flare. If there's one thing I've been learning about Madison Smith, it's that she doesn't like to be told what to do... and another thing? She hates losing.

I raise my hands. "How about we make this more interesting? The loser will be dunked in the dunking booth."

“Oh, I’m never getting wet,” she declares, her chin lifted in defiance.

A beat passes, and then her eyes widen as she realizes the unintended innuendo. “I mean—I’m not going to lose. So, I won’t be getting dunked. In water. Fully clothed. Definitely not wet.” She’s rambling now, and based on her glare—she’s not used to it—even though I’ve heard her ramble a couple of times already.

I lean in close, my lips almost brushing the shell of her ear, “Never say never.”

She shivers, her breath catching audibly. For a moment, we’re suspended in the tension, the rest of the world falling away. But then my mother steps forward, clears her throat, and the spell is broken.

“I’m going to check on the pie contest with Ava,” my mom says, her eyes twinkling with that knowing look I’ve seen too many times. “You two have fun with your little competition.”

As she saunters off, I fight the urge to roll my eyes. Moms, right? But then Maddie turns to me, her cheeks flushed, and her chin lifted in that stubborn way of hers.

"You're going down, Navy SEAL Man," she declares, all fire and bravado.

I can't help it. A slow, wicked grin spreads across my face as my eyes rake over her body, taking in every curve, every inch. "Down, huh?" I drawl, my voice rough with suggestion.

She blinks, then shakes her head, a reluctant smile tugging at her lips. "Not... down... I mean... you know what I mean," she stammers, a bubble of laughter escaping her. "And I can't believe you didn't tell me Lady Grey is your mom! I... those books... You saw the cover. And I told you about the orgasms, the..."

"Please," I groan, feeling the heat creep up my neck. My mind's caught in a tug-of-war between mortification and arousal. "Let's not... Mom and orgasms don't belong in the same zip code, let alone the same sentence."

Maddie's eyes widen, and she bursts into laughter. "Your face!"

I scrub a hand over my face, trying to school my expression into something less... conflicted. "Glad I could provide some entertainment," I grunt, but I can't keep the corner of my mouth from twitching upward.

"So," she says, eyes dancing with humor. "Does this mean you've never read her books?"

"That's classified information, Princess," I rasp, leaning in close enough to catch the scent of her shampoo. "And if you know what's good for you, you'll drop this line of questioning. Immediately."

The air between us crackles with tension, equal parts playful and heated. Maddie's still grinning, but there's a flush creeping up her neck that tells me she's not as composed as she's trying to appear.

"Or what, SEAL Man?" she challenges, tilting her chin up. "You'll make me walk the plank?"

Unlike so many others, she doesn't shy away from my past. Maybe she doesn't know everything I've gone through, but she sees the scars, the tattoos, and she didn't ask for a one-way ticket out of town, and she doesn't make me feel like I have to talk or hide or pretend to be someone I'm not.

I arch an eyebrow. "Don't tempt me. I might just make you walk the plank... and then we'll both go down."

There's a pause. Something in the air shifts. And then another burst of giggles. "That's a line your mom would write! You know what I mean?"

That laugh... damn. It's true. It's real. It hits me like the g-force in Monaco's infamous Fairmont Hairpin—gut-wrenching, exhilarating, and addictive as hell. My grin softens into something more genuine, something that feels dangerously close to affection. I want to hear her laugh more. I want to be the one making her laugh, but it's more than that—I want her to be happy.

"Oh, I know exactly what you mean. But trust me, whoever goes down will enjoy every second of it..." I pause, letting the tension build. "I'm talking about the dunking booth, of course."

Maddie inches forward, a challenge in her eyes and in her voice. "Of course," she says, her tone dripping with sarcasm. "But let's see who wins first, shall we? I hope you brought your water wings, SEAL Man."

CHAPTER 15—MADDIE

Becca: Did you say you're entering a crab-eating contest? You never want to pick a lobster at the restaurant because you're worried about them. How is that going to work?
Maddie: It's starting in two minutes. I've got this.

WE'VE GATHERED QUITE a crowd. And I don't know why, but that makes me even more tense. I can do this. I can eat more crabs than him. We're both not from here, and I've been watching videos on how to do it. Those are crabs. Not some sort of alien I need to pick and eat.

Even though I'm still unclear on what the mustard is and whether or not I should eat it. Or why anyone eats it.

"The rules are clear," Jevonte announces into a microphone, and is the sun beating on us even more? I feel a bead of sweat sliding down my spine. The salty scent of Old Bay mingles with the tang of my own perspiration, making my nose itch and my eyes water. I try to ignore the discomfort, focusing all my energy on cracking open the stubborn shell in front of me.

I glance at Damian, who is sitting next to me, looking relaxed, but he's not fooling me. He's tapping his foot, and his jaw is clenched. Yep. I'm getting under his skin.

"You didn't think I'd follow through, did you?" I whisper to him, and his smile turns into a deep chuckle. It transforms his face, softening the hard edges, making him look younger, more approachable. For a moment, I forget about the article, about my carefully cultivated image. I just want to hear that sound again. To be the cause of it. It's a dangerous thought. One that has butterflies racing in my chest.

Stupid butterflies.

His lips shouldn't fascinate me that much. Yet, I'm still staring at them when he says, "Or maybe I counted on it." He doesn't glance around the crowd. His sole focus is on me. "I don't think you're ready for this."

Jevonte continues explaining the rules, and I try very hard to stop getting distracted by Mr. Muscles in front of me. "We're following the rules of the crab derby contest for this."

"The crab derby?" I frown.

Damian tilts his head. "I guess you haven't brushed up on your Maryland stories."

Luckily for me, Jevonte adds, "You have to eat three crabs clean to win, and yes, of course, no mallet!"

"No mallet?" I croak. That might complicate things. Like how am I supposed to eat without mallets?

And what am I not eating? Am I eating everything?

But before I can ask any questions, three crabs are brought to our table covered with paper, and someone blows into a horn. Damian starts with a precision that almost has me in awe... how can his fingers do that?

I can do the same. Some of the videos I've watched must have prepared me for it. So, I got at it, pulling a leg out and knocking it on the table to try to open it. Parts of the shell flies everywhere, and I'm pretty sure I've got Old Bay in places Old Bay really shouldn't be.

Damian whistles when he sees me go at the second crab. "Not bad, Big City girl. Not bad."

But as I crack another crab, the shell pokes into the inside of my palm, and I wince. "Ouch." With the Old Bay, it burns and burns and burns. The sharp sting of the cut radiates through my hand, the pain mixing with the frustration and embarrassment of potentially losing the contest. I try to shake it off, determined to push through, but the burn only intensifies.

I shake it again. I can continue, but Damian's gaze focuses on me, and he jumps up. "She cut herself!" He calls out, waving to stop. "We have to stop, she cut herself."

"I'm not done. I can continue. I'm not going to lose." An image of me trying out for the soccer team in middle school floats to my mind. The snickers of the kids when they realized I didn't really know what I was doing. The tears I hid in the bathroom. The way my throat felt like sandpaper. Like now. This is why I joined the yearbook club and then followed with the newspaper club and debate team in high school. It was easier to report on the stories than to be the story.

Easier and less hurtful.

Damian reaches out to grab my hand. I pull it away, but he grabs it again. "Let me see."

He's gentle. And his touch doesn't recoil me. Far from it. When was the last time someone took care of me? I can't remember. And right now, with Damian blowing on my hand to see the wound, his breath warm and soothing against my skin, I feel like I'm in a cocoon and yet way too exposed at the same time. I want to lean into his touch, to let myself be vulnerable, but a part of me is still holding back, afraid of what it might mean.

"Let's just say you won," I croak out, and Damian shakes his head. People have moved away toward the stage where there's a band playing, and he helps me up.

"You're not getting into that water with that wound. That could get infected. That could..." He shakes his head. "Let me get the first aid kit."

But he doesn't let go of my hand as we head toward the firefighter booth. He grabs what he needs and slowly cleans the wound. That crab really got me.

"You were very good at that crab-eating contest," Damian mutters.

"YouTube for the win."

"It's going to sting a little." And when he dabs on the wound, I flinch, the pain sharp and bright. But Damian's touch is gentle, his fingers brushing against my skin in a way that sends shivers down my spine. "So, you say you like serial killer movies," he continues. "I think they're overrated."

"Overrated? Please!" And as I go on a diatribe about how the genre has gone through so many changes, the importance of jump scares and psychological fear, Damian just listens—until I realize he's done cleaning and bandaging my hand.

He leans in, close, so close, his cologne becomes part of the air, and my breath must take a detour between my lungs and my lips. "I actually love those movies, too," he whispers—his breath warm on my skin.

"Thank you, um, for distracting me."

His green eyes lock with mine—until the horn rings again.

"I'll be at the booth. Try to get me into the water... if you can."

And I laugh.

As soon as he's out of sight, I lean against a tree. I know better than to think this meant anything, anything at all. But it's nice for once to have someone take care of me.

His mom strolls my way. "Look at him," she says with a bright smile. "You know he's always been so careful to not show others he cares. Maybe it's because we adopted him. But he always cared so much." She pauses as if she wants to tell me more, but thinks better of it and two seconds later, she slaps her thigh with her hand. "Oh my god, I have a new idea for a book." She winces. "But I don't have my phone. And I need to record the plot, or I'm going to forget. I..."

"I have my recorder. Why don't you take it if you want?" And as I pull out my recorder from my purse, Damian glares our way, his expression a mix of suspicion and something else I can't quite decipher. Is he worried I'm going to use this moment for a story? Does he feel exposed, vulnerable? I want to reassure him, to tell him that I would never betray his trust like that. But before I can say anything, he turns away, his shoulders tense.

What did I do now?

CHAPTER 16—DAMIAN

Subject line: Barkey Hey, Damian. Just wanted to let you know that Barkey has really been opening up, and we think a foster might really help him. Do you know someone who might be interested?
Let me know.

MY FISTS CLENCH. ANGER courses through me like lava. It takes everything I've got not to storm over and rip that recorder from Madison's hands. I force myself to turn away.

Distance. I need distance before I do something stupid.

Mom has already been too trusting once. Granted, it was with a so-called fan online who ended up spreading lies about her. But I remember her feeling helpless.

I glance down at my phone, the screen still glowing with the website I stumbled upon. *Not-Crabby-News.* I thought it was supposed to be some kind of feel-good local news site, a celebration of all things Swans Cove. But what I'm seeing is nothing but sensationalized bullshit, a toxic wasteland of gossip and exploitation.

My stomach turns as I scroll. Each article is worse than the last. People's lives, dragged into the spotlight for clicks and cash. Disgusting.

And Madison... I can't believe I let myself start to trust her. To think that maybe, just maybe, she was different. But here she is, cozying up to my mother, probably trying to dig up some dirt for her next big scoop. The thought makes my blood boil, my vision blurring at the edges.

Because my mom has already dealt with enough: invasive questions about her personal life, probing who she loves, and forcing her to share parts of herself she wanted to keep private. I won't let Madison do the same.

With a steady hand and unwavering resolve, I pull up Carlos's contact and press call. "Hey," I say, my voice tight with suppressed intensity, each word measured and deliberate. "I need you to do me a favor. Rally everyone to the dunking booth and announce that Lady Grey is about to dunk her son."

It's a cheap trick, a way to cut Madison's little interview short. But right now, I don't care. All I care about is keeping my mother safe, keeping Swans Cove out of the crosshairs of some gossip-hungry reporter.

I end the call and shove my phone back into my pocket; my jaw clenched so tight it aches. I can feel the curious stares, the whispers of the crowd as they start to gather around the dunking booth. But I ignore them, my gaze fixed on the horizon, on the sun-dappled water of the bay.

I'll do whatever it takes to protect what's mine, to shield the people I love from the vultures circling overhead. And if that means going toe-to-toe with Madison Smith, so be it.

I'm ready for a fight.

WHAT I DIDN'T EXPECT was my mother deciding that Madison should have the honor.

Because, of course she does.

The crowd's pressing in, their noise grating on my nerves. My heart's racing like I'm about to jump out of a plane, and I have to remind myself to breathe. In, out. In, out. The mix of funnel cakes and sweat isn't doing my stomach any favors.

Whole damn town must be here, closing in. The rough wood of this booth digs into my back. I've been in tighter spots, but this? This is different.

Never told anyone, but I get why Alessandro hates enclosed spaces. I always kept that to myself. My armor's supposed to be solid. Titanium, not carbon fiber.

That window Mom installed in my room years back, the one I could leave open at night? Yeah, I get why now. The memory of cool air helps, but it's not enough.

I shift on this bench, muscles tense. This was supposed to be a challenge. Now? I'm not so sure what I'm trying to prove.

And why does it feel like Maddie's got something to do with all this?

"Come on!" Someone yells with laughter in their voice.

And Madison stands there—like she's hesitating. "Are you sure about this?" She calls out like she's the one throwing the gauntlet back at me. "You were a gentleman during the crab-eating contest." And there's a bite in her tone—like I was the one playing a role.

Her words are like salt in an open wound, stinging and sharp. I clench my jaw, tasting bile at the back of my throat.

"Oh, come on," I yell out, my voice raw and jagged. "How about you cut the crap—maybe that's a story you could write about for your Not-Crabby-News..."

The words hang between us, challenging and accusing. Maddie flinches, surprise and hurt flashing in her eyes. But I can't bring myself to care, not when I feel like I'm coming apart, my walls crumbling. It's not fear. Never fear.

Is that the same look on Madison's face?

"Fine," she snaps, grabbing the ball. My stomach tightens as she aims straight for the target.

The crowd roars as I hit the cold water. It's familiar and shocking all at once, exactly what I need.

As I surface and climb the ladder, I catch Maddie's eyes on me.

Yeah, my shirt's clinging to every muscle, and she's definitely noticing. Can't say I mind.

Lydia and Sereen rush over with a towel, but I'm more focused on Maddie slipping away.

Of course she is.

I head straight for Mom, ready to lay out exactly what's been going on. But her eyes widen, and she purses her lips in that way that always spells trouble. It's not anger—it's worse. Disappointment.

"Oh, honey," she starts, and I brace myself. "Sometimes you're not protecting others; you're just hiding yourself. Open your eyes." Her hand on my face is gentle, but her words hit hard. "Maddie was just helping me record book notes. I don't know what you think you saw, but it wasn't about me."

Well, shit.

CHAPTER 17—MADDIE

Becca: Did you see that horse therapy farm in Hollow Bay? It's close to you. Also... Chase got injured in today's game, and he's out for the rest of the season. Those two pieces of information may be related. Love you.

WHY IS THERE A BARBWIRE tightening around my throat? Anyone? Or maybe it's a crab leg poking at me. That's it. It's the revenge of the crab.

It's not just that. Everyone heard what he said.

E-very-one.

Oh, I heard the gasps when he growled at me from the dunk booth, and the chuckles. Saw one or two pitying glances, too.

And here I was, thinking that we were coming to some sort of truce. Clearly, my bullshit radar is off. Broken. Useless.

I fumble with my keys, my hands shaking so badly it takes me three tries to get the door open.

As soon as I'm inside, I kick it shut and slide to the floor. The rough wood scrapes against my back, splinters catching on my thin skirt as my butt hits the ground. Cold water seeps through the fabric, soaking my panties and sending a chill up my spine.

I guess I'm getting wet after all.

Why is there water here? I slide as I get up... the flood alarm isn't beeping, but there's a poodle of water by the sink, too. And there's a post it on the counter.

The pipes in the kitchen had an issue. Sorry about the mess. Paul said he'll contact you about the B&B...

Johnny (Plumber)

Shaking my head, I let out another heavy sigh that sounds a lot like a strangled sob, the sound echoing in the empty apartment.

What was I thinking, coming here? Thinking I could start over, prove myself in this tiny town where everyone knows everyone else's business? It's not only that none of the stores on Main Street deliver food 24/7 or that there is no noise in the night. It's just... people actually look at me. But they're not looking at me like they want to get to know me. What am I even thinking? I rub my temples with my index fingers.

A muffled meow breaks through my spiraling thoughts, and my heart leaps into my throat. "Fluffy!" I scramble to my feet, my pulse pounding in my ears as I nearly slip on the wet floor.

I throw open the bedroom door, terrified of what I might find. But there's Fluffy, laid out on my bed like he's Kate Winslet in Titanic—that famous, "Draw me like one of your French girls." He's giving me a look that says, "What do you want hooman? How dare you disturb my rest?"

Relief crashes over me like a wave, so intense it makes my knees go weak.

He's okay.

He's totally fine.

I'm okay.

I'm.... so not totally fine.

I slump against the doorframe, running a trembling hand through my hair. The damp wood beneath my feet is a stark reminder of the chaos that seems to follow me wherever I go. It's not just my love life and career that are in shambles—even my supposed refuge, my home, is falling apart. The flooded apartment feels like a physical manifestation of the upheaval in my life, and I can't help but wonder if I'll ever find solid ground again.

My WhatsApp ringtone makes me jump and I answer it without even checking who's calling. I'm definitely not hoping for Mr. Hot and Grumpy to be reaching out.

That would be stupid.

"Hello?" I sound super upbeat. Too upbeat. No one ever sounds that upbeat.

Especially with the mascara smudged all over my eyes. The camera doesn't lie. I look like a mess.

"What's wrong?" Becca has her no-nonsense voice, and because she knows me, she adds, "Did you see my text about Chase?"

"No... is he okay?" She winces, and I can see "crappy news" written all over her face. Whatever happened, people who hate me will despise me even more. Great. And part of me wonders if maybe all this attention didn't distract him. He hated the spotlight on him—and I didn't listen. I plowed my way through. My throat tightens.

"Maddie-love, I'm so sorry."

Maddie-love, that's what she used to call me in middle school when we had sleepovers. The nickname she'd use after I told her about the Ice Princess. We'd lie on the scratchy carpet of her basement, the scent of sage and melted candle wax wafting from the paranormal investigation equipment her parents stored in the back room. I never could shake the feeling that those EMF meters and spirit boxes were picking up on my secrets like they could sense the skeletons in my closet. The goals I didn't yet reach. The feeling of not being enough. Never being enough. Of pretending so much until I made it that I forgot who I am.

Her parents didn't realize that Becca was either getting picked on at school, kids making ghost noises at her or asking if she could talk to their pets' ancestors.

On Halloween, though? They would all cram up outside, waiting to see all the wild displays her parents put on.

"Mads?" She asks again.

"Everything?" I croak out, my voice cracking. "Like everything-everything." And there we go. Tear number one is closely followed by tear number two, about to pass it on the track of its life.

Becca sighs. "Those stupid Hallmark movies, making small-town life look all cute and quirky. They never show the gossip or the judgment or the..."

As Becca's voice washes over me, I close my eyes and let my head thump back against the door. What am I going to do now?

What-Would-A-Winner-Do? That has been my motto ever since I didn't get a main role in my ballet showcase when I was ten. At the time, I was still happy to twirl on stage, but

I looked into the audience and saw my parents chatting with other parents. Not watching me.

Afterward, they told my sister she was a winner and how proud they were of her for clinching a title role in a play. They barely acknowledged me. Not even a pat on the back. "Aren't you proud of Rose, too? She's going to be a star." That's what they said. And yes, I was proud of my sister, but I had fun on stage, too.

If I wasn't first... then I was forgotten. Or at least, that's how it felt. That's when I knew I had to be the best, always, to be worthy of attention. To be worthy of love.

And here I am, trying to prove myself again in a place where everyone knows everyone else's business. Trying to start over when all I feel is the crushing weight of unmet expectations. What was I thinking?

"What would a winner do?" I murmur out loud, and Becca winces.

"You're still doing that?" She asks me with a worried tone that wraps around my chest because I can't be disappointing her, too.

"It's been working for me," I remind her. "I could have lost my shit and my career after Chase but look at me." I pause, straightening my shoulders and wiping the tears from my cheeks. "I mean... I'm working on something now. I won't let Mr. Hot and Grumpy derail me."

"Mr. Hot and Grumpy. Your neighbor, right?"

"Yep. He's definitely not an old grandpa."

"An old grandpa?"

"I told you I thought he was a grandpa. Or a grandma. But he's not. And he's holding a grudge..."

"But he's hot and grumpy. Maybe he's rebound-you-need-an-orgasm hot and grumpy?"

An image of Damian flashes back to my mind. As he hauled himself away from the dunking booth—all those muscles rippling under his wet shirt, water cascading down his chiseled features. I couldn't tear my eyes away from the way his clothes clung to every curve and plane of his body, like a second skin. Heat pooled low in my belly, a flush creeping up my neck as I imagined what it would feel like to have all that intense attention focused on me, to have those strong hands exploring my curves...

I shake my head, trying to dislodge the thought. But it's like a seed has been planted, and I can't stop my mind from wandering down that more delicious than caramel brulee ice-cream path. What would it be like to be the sole focus of a man like Damian? To let go of control and surrender to pure, unadulterated pleasure?

I squirm in my seat, my thighs clenching together as a bolt of desire shoots through me. I can almost feel the ghost of his touch on my skin, the rasp of his stubble against my neck as he—

"Earth to Maddie!" Becca's voice snaps me out of my fantasy, and I feel my face flame even hotter.

"Sorry, what were you saying?" I ask, trying to sound nonchalant. But from the

knowing smirk on Becca's face, I'm not fooling anyone.

"You were thinking about that orgasm, weren't you?"

"Way to veer off-topic."

She shrugs. "All I'm saying is that you might want to let go, hold on to the bedpost, and let yourself be worshipped for once."

"Becca!"

"When is the last time you got a good...."

"I swear, if you say 'dicking,' I'm changing your contact name to Becking."

"All I'm saying is that you made sure Chase was happy in bed—and you made sure he didn't feel inadequate..."

"He wasn't."

"But when did you last see stars?"

"Outside my window, using my very trusted vibrator; thank you so much for asking."

"Probably after reading a romance novel..."

"Talking about romance novels..."

"Look who's changing topic now."

"I met Lady Grey."

"You did what?" She squeals.

"And Mr. Hot-And-Grumpy is her son."

Becca fans herself with her hand. "So, tell me, what would a winner do?"

"You're using this against me?"

"For you, babe. Always for you."

"The winner wouldn't let this setback derail her completely. She'd get up and write that crab feast article, and then she'd go to that self-defense class with her head high."

"There you go," Becca pauses. A long pause that tells me she's not done handing out Becca-ism. "That, and she'd also remember that she doesn't need to win to be loved."

I take a deep, shuddering breath, Becca's words echoing in my head. I want to believe her, I do. But it's hard to shake the feeling that I'll always be on the outside looking in. I glance at my phone, at the depressingly short list of contacts. Besides Becca, one of my former colleagues, and my sister, no one's reached out since I moved here. Okay, Mom and Dad did ask me if Chase had changed his mind... and not-so-subtly mentioned me changing my career into academia.

I sometimes went out with friends back in the city. Chase and I would host parties. I worked so many hours. And when I didn't work, I did research on future articles.

Here, no one really talks to me. Granted, I've been here for less than a week. But still...

Just silence. And living in the city, I'm not used to it.

And like that teddy bear called BooBuddy Becca's parents had on display—I'm supposed to react to changes in my environment, to gauge the temperature, to know how to interact with people. And yet... I still feel... lonely sometimes.

I sigh, my breath hitching in my throat. Becca's right; I can't let this setback derail me completely. I have to keep going, keep pushing, even if it feels like I'm screaming into the void.

I'll write that crab feast article, and I'll go to that self-defense class. I'll show this town and myself what Maddie Smith is made of.

But as for not needing to win to be loved? I'm not there yet. I'm not sure I'll ever be.

CHAPTER 18—DAMIAN

Alessandro: Wow. Impressive take on the senior and not-so-seniors' defense and mobility class...
Damian: I am charming.
Alessandro: You have your moments.
Alessandro: How is Maddie?
Damian: ...

MY FISTS CONNECT WITH the leathered punching bag again and again, each impact sending a jolt of pain through my knuckles and up my arms. The bag swings wildly, the chains rattling in protest as I pour all my frustration, all my confusion, into every punch. Sweat drips into my eyes, my lungs burning with each ragged breath, but I don't stop. I can't stop.

Not when Madison Smith's voice is burrowed under my skin like splinters. She started a podcast—because, of course, she did. The rumor mill—aka Aunt Locelli—mentioned she thought it might be a good way to bring Swans Cove to people all around the world.

Another one of Maddie's let's-get-out-of-here ideas, I'm sure.

For someone who may never have gone to a crab feast? My three tips would be simple:

- Old Bay everything;

- Mallets for the win;

- Enjoy.

She didn't enjoy herself. And that was my fault. I tried to knock on her door Sunday night to apologize—but she wasn't home. I haven't seen her all week. Part of me thought she actually left—but Aisling told me Maddie has been staying at the B&B while the landlord was repainting her place.

I put my music even louder than usual to drown out the noises in my head.

The Gazette is also happy to announce the winner of the shelter "Name a Pet" game. The winner is Ava. She named a dog Loki, and that dog ended up going home with her, Alessandro, and Aisling. I've heard from little Ava herself that she's baking dog cookies for Loki.

Loki has found a home—where he feels safe, happy, and secure. He's learning to trust and be himself in all the ways that matter. So I feel like they're all winners.

Because finding a home is everything.

Thump. Thump. Thump.

It's like she crawled inside my mind and put down in words feelings I didn't even know existed.

I feel seen. Understood.

Like I'm a shelter dog.

Always looking for a place to belong. Always hoping that someone will see past the scars and the rough edges and choose me.

Choose me.

How many times did I fall asleep muttering those words to myself as a damn lullaby?

When I first landed in the foster care system, I hoped for my parents to come back. Or for my Aunt Kelly to take me in. No one did.

And in that first foster home? They had taken three other kids—and you could tell those kids were scared of someone taking their place. Everyone was trying to survive, it seemed now. So, they made fun of me for my tears, my crooked smile, my skinny frame. Well, they should see me now. I still have my crooked smile; don't let feelings overwhelm me—and that skinny frame is gone.

I throw myself back into the workout, my muscles screaming with each punch. I may be lost in my own head, but as soon as the door creaks open, I'm on my guard, aware, and whirl around.

"What did that punching bag ever do to you?" Alessandro frowns.

I stiffen, my jaw clenching as I turn to face him. He's got that look on his face, the one that says he knows me too well. That's his "what-the-fuck-Damian" face.

I force a smile I don't feel. "Just working out some tension," I say, my voice rough. "You know how it is."

Alessandro frowns, his eyes searching mine. For a moment, I'm terrified he's going to push, that he's going to make me confront the truth I'm trying so hard to ignore.

But he just nods, clapping me on the shoulder. "Well, when you're done beating the hell out of that bag, we need to talk about the new class schedule."

I nod, relief and disappointment warring in my gut. Part of me wants him to push, to force me to face the feelings Maddie's words have stirred up. But the other part, the part that's been hurt too many times, is just grateful for the reprieve.

"I'll be there in a minute," I say, turning back to the bag. "Just need to finish this set."

I can feel Alessandro's eyes on me for a long moment before he turns to go. And as the door swings shut behind him, I let out a groan.

Just a few more punches. A few more minutes of blissful, mindless exertion. And then I'll put Madison Smith and her too-perceptive words out of my mind.

I hope.

Alessandro pokes his head out. "I confirmed Maddie for tomorrow's class—just thought you might want to know so you can punch that bag a few more times instead of realizing you have it bad for the woman."

I clench my jaw even more to not blurt something stupid out, and give him the finger instead.

He chuckles but still gives me a tilt of his head—his signature, think-about-it-man move. Never mind that he had sworn off all relationships until that baking show we worked on as security.

Until he stepped into Swans Cove.

I turn back to the punching bag, losing myself in the movement again—but it's Madison's tempting body I see, her laughter I hear, the way her skin felt against mine when I took care of that cut, the hurt in her eyes at the dunking booth...

Damn Alessandro and his former Navy Seal's perceptive eyes. Damn Madison Smith and her podcast.

Damn my own stupid heart that keeps on wanting more despite knowing better.

I slam my fist into the bag, the impact jarring up my arm. Fuck, that's good. Pain's simple. Honest. Unlike the mess in my head.

I breathe in deep, the smell of sweat and leather filling my lungs. It's a familiar scent, a comforting one.

In here, I'm in control. In here, I know who I am.

But out there? With Maddie? It's like all my hard-won control goes out the window. She's like sand in my gears—irritating as hell, gets everywhere, and I can't seem to shake her out. Makes me want things I've got no business wanting. Dangerous doesn't begin to cover it.

I hit the bag again, harder this time. The tape on my hands is starting to fray, but I don't stop. I can't. Because stopping means thinking, and thinking means facing

the truth.

What if no one chooses me again?

After one more punch, I head into the office, rubbing the back of my head with the towel, and cross my arms over my chest.

Alessandro raises one infuriating eyebrow. "I read your proposal about the kids-be-yourself class. Maybe we can have Emma and Carlos look it over for both the education and therapy angles."

"Yeah, that makes sense," I mutter, avoiding his gaze. "Having an educator and a therapist check it out could help."

Alessandro nods, then hesitates. "There's something else. Have you listened to Maddie's other podcast episodes?"

I tense, my jaw clenching. "No, just the crab feast one. Why?"

"Well," Alessandro says, leaning forward, "the one with Ryan is getting a lot of attention. Having a former NFL player and local celebrity talk about us has been getting a lot of national response. He had great things to say about our mobility program."

My heart rate picks up, but I force my voice to remain neutral. "And?"

"And it's bringing in new inquiries. Maybe even some potential investors." Alessandro's eyes are searching my face. "Could help with the expansion costs. Might even let us offer more scholarships for the youth programs."

I grunt, not trusting myself to speak. Part of me wants to feel relieved, excited even. But another part, the part that's been hurt before, whispers caution. After all, Maddie's leaving soon. We can't build our future on someone who's already got one foot out the door.

"Funny how things work out, huh?" Alessandro adds, that knowing look back in his eyes.

I roll mine in response. "Don't start. Just because you found your happily ever after doesn't mean everyone needs one."

"Also..." Alessandro pauses, a hint of a smirk on his face. "I heard you sent flowers to Maddie. Good call."

I roll my eyes. "Of course you heard. Is anything in this town a secret? I'm surprised she didn't write an article in the Gazette about it..."

"Did you actually read her articles?" He taps his fingers on his thigh, watching me. I recognize that look—it's the one that tries to dig deep inside you.

"You're way too interested in this," I mutter before deflecting. "How's Loki doing? Acclimating okay?"

Alessandro shakes his head, chuckling. "Changing the subject won't change the fact that I know you, man."

He clears his throat, his fingers tracing the picture of Aisling, him, and Ava on his desk. "Look, you know how I always thought I wasn't built for happily ever after? How I kept everyone at arm's length because I was scared of getting hurt or hurting them?"

I nod, tensing. I can sense where this is going.

"Well, with Aisling, I learned that was all bullshit." His voice softens. "We're not protecting anyone by running away. Real strength is in staying, in being vulnerable, in letting someone see all of you—the good and the bad."

I run a hand through my hair, frustration building inside me. "It's not that easy, man. Maddie and I... we're complicated. She's leaving soon anyway..."

Alessandro gives me a look. "Maybe. But don't you think it's time to reassess some of those rules you've set for yourself?"

I grunt, not wanting to engage. But something makes me admit, "She's got guts, I'll give her that. And yes, based on what I keep hearing, she seems to genuinely care about the stories she tells."

"Sounds like someone else I know," Alessandro says with a knowing glint in his eye, raising his hands when I grunt.

As Alessandro leaves, I find myself staring at the picture on his desk. Him, Aisling, and Ava—a family.

I already have mine. And I've never allowed myself to want or even consider anything more.

I shake my head, pushing away the unwelcome thoughts. That's not for me. It's safer this way. Easier.

So why does it suddenly feel so damn lonely?

Not wanting to deal with those thoughts, I go back inside the gym, because nothing says I got my shit together like a workout that leaves me breathless.

After thirty more minutes, I land one final, punishing blow to the bag. No. I know better. I have to know better.

Unwrapping my hands, I slump onto the bench, exhaustion seeping into my bones. My phone pings—probably Alessandro with another smart-ass comment. But when I glance at the screen, it's Alessandro with a link to an article written by Maddie a couple of years ago. Some over-the-top piece, no doubt.

Except it's not.

It's an article about Court Appointed Special Advocates (CASA) in foster care, by Madison Smith.

My thumb hovers over the link. I shouldn't. I know I shouldn't. But before I can talk myself out of it, I'm reading.

Damn if she doesn't nail it. The importance of having someone in your corner when the world's turned its back on you. It's like she's crawled inside my head and picked every thought I thought I had kept hidden, which is both impressive and fucking terrifying. Juliet—My CASA—helped me so much.

For a moment, I forget to breathe.

This isn't some fluff piece cranked out by a caffeine junkie looking for their next byline. This... this has teeth. And heart. Didn't see that coming.

I toss the phone aside, running a hand over my face. Shit. Just when I thought I had Maddie Smith figured out, she goes and does this. Makes me want to know more. Makes me wonder what other depths are hiding behind that smile.

But it doesn't change anything. Can't change anything. She's still leaving, and I still have my rules.

Even if those rules are starting to feel a hell of a lot like excuses...

CHAPTER 19—MADDIE

Rose: Love the podcast episodes! Oh, and I saw about Chase... Tried to call you. Also, Mom is thinking about signing you up for a new dating app.

HITTING THE GYM USED to be my go-to for endorphins and stress relief. A surefire way to clear my head, like a final girl outrunning the masked killer in the last act. But now? Not so much.

The cause of my impending cardio catastrophe? None other than Damian Mack, standing in the middle of the room like some Greek god statue come to life, if Greek statues wore gray sweatpants and had scars and tattoos. He's surrounded by a gaggle of swooning Swans Cove seniors asking for a preview of the class.

As I watch him demonstrate a self-defense move, my inner reporter kicks into overdrive. Every flex of his muscles, every patient explanation, every bark of laughter at a senior's joke—it's all primo material for a feature piece. "Local Adonis Teaches Grannies How to Kick Butt While Stealing Hearts."

His hands, the same ones that so gently tended to my crab feast battle wound, now guide Mrs. Henderson through a wrist escape. Those calloused fingers, capable of such tenderness and strength have me wondering where else he might apply that dexterity. And when he uses that commanding tone to correct someone's stance? Let's just say I'm imagining him using it in very different circumstances. Circumstances that would make all my favorite authors blush.

And I'm not thinking about Lady Grey because she's his mom, and that's just weird.

But it's not just the physical stuff that's got me tied up in knots. It's the way little Ava's face lights up when she sees him, the fierce loyalty Alessandro shows him, the quiet way he shows up for his friends without fanfare. He probably doesn't even realize how the whole town talks about him—their not-even homegrown hero with a heart of gold.

I swear Mrs. Norris is one step away from asking for his autograph—on her chest. "Just in case," I hear her titter, and I roll my eyes so hard I'm surprised they don't get stuck in the back of my head. Great. Now I'm picturing the headline: "Reporter's Eyeballs Stuck After Epic Eye-Roll, Local Hunk to Blame."

Pulitzer, here I come. Not.

If only my heart would stop trying to burst out of my chest like I'm in some B-grade horror flick. But with Damian in the room, looking like that, being... well, him? Fat chance. I'm in trouble, deep trouble. And the worst part? A tiny, traitorous part of me is enjoying every second of it.

Aunt Locelli sidles up to me, her cane tapping against the floor. "Oh, dear, it's so lovely to see you. How has the Bed and

Breakfast been treating you? It's been so long since we had one here in Swans Cove."

"It's been wonderful," I reply, pasting on my best small-talk smile. And it's true—the B&B has been a cozy refuge. But I still feel like an outsider looking in, a tourist on the fringes of this tight-knit town.

Aunt Locelli leans closer, her voice dropping to a stage whisper. "Glad to hear it. Also, did I hear correctly? You're planning on leaving us? Paul told me your rent is now month-to-month. Not that he could really argue, with all the damage to your clothes and everything. You could have gotten him into trouble, you know."

I feel Damian's gaze boring into me, hot and heavy. Did he hear her? Well, two can play that game.

"Yes, I am planning on leaving soon," I say, pitching my voice just a touch louder than necessary. "The assignment was a one-month gig at the Gazette. Something to see if we were a good match."

"A good match, huh?" Aunt Locelli glances at Damian, who's standing close by. And I can see the matchmaking look in her eyes—my mom gets the same one. I really don't need someone else trying to tell me l need to make myself available for love.

"Actually," I continue, remembering my conversation with Ed and making sure to stay on the topic at hand. "I'm not even covering this class. Ed's coming to the next one to write about it himself."

"So you're here just for yourself?" Aunt Locelli's eyebrows shoot up like she's auditioning for a soap opera.

I nod. "Ed's got this idea that I should experience Swans Cove without my reporter goggles on. Says the best stories come when you're living life, not just scribbling about it from the sidelines."

I roll my eyes, but there's no real annoyance behind it. "Plus, after my stellar performance at the crab feast, he probably thinks I need all the self-defense training I can get. You know, in case the crabs decide to seek revenge."

Aunt Locelli cracks up, her laugh echoing through the gym. "Oh, honey, you're a riot. And speaking of riots..." She nods towards Damian, who's busy flexing his muscles. I mean, setting up equipment. "Word on the street is that our instructor there has been quite taken with your podcast. Bringing in some fresh blood for the school, from what I hear."

Wait, what? Damian's been listening to my podcast? And it's actually helping the school? My heart does a little tap dance in my chest, but I force my face to remain neutral. "Oh, that's... neat," I manage, my voice only slightly strangled. "Glad it's been useful."

Real smooth, Maddie. Pulitzer Prize-winning commentary right there.

Aunt Locelli's eyes sparkle like she's just uncovered the scoop of the century. "And those tulips he sent you? Honey, in the short time Damian's been here, I've never seen him go full Hallmark movie before. Our broody instructor's got it bad."

I resist the urge to facepalm. Of course the town gossip mill is running overtime on this. "The flowers were just an apology," I mutter, feeling my cheeks heat up. "For the crab feast fiasco. Nothing more."

"Sure, dear," Aunt Locelli pats my arm, her tone screaming *I don't believe you for a second.* "And I'm secretly Swans Cove's Batman."

I roll my eyes, but my gaze traitorously darts to Damian. It doesn't help that Damian is suddenly right there, close enough to touch. Close enough to smell the clean, woodsy scent of his cologne. I clench my hands at my sides, resisting the urge to reach out and run my fingers over the ridges of his abs.

Get it together, Maddie. This isn't one of Lady Grey's steamier scenes. This is real life.

But try telling that to my treacherous body, which seems to have missed the memo. Every cell feels attuned to Damian's presence, every nerve ending sparking like a live wire.

I think back to the flowers he sent me at the B&B, the note scrawled in his strong, slanting hand. "I'm sorry," it said. Two little words, but they lodged themselves under my skin, a thorn I can't seem to shake loose.

I'm sure the gossip mill is churning at full speed, speculating on what exactly he's sorry for. If they only knew the half of it.

"The defense instructor would love for everyone to gather," Damian announces, his voice cutting through my spiraling thoughts. "Let's do some warm-ups first."

As the class assembles, I take a deep breath, squaring my shoulders. I can do this. I can make it through one class without jumping Damian's bones or revealing just how much he gets under my skin.

Easy peasy, lemon squeezy. Right?

EASY SWEATY, LEMON crappy is more like it. I can feel the heat of Damian's body behind me, the whisper of his breath on my neck as he corrects my stance. It's like being in one of those slasher flicks, where you know the killer is right there, but you can't see him. Except instead of fear, what I'm feeling is decidedly more... tingly.

Oh, he's a great instructor. Wonderful. Funny and sweet and encouraging. But he's also riding me. And not in the way he did in my dreams last night, all hard muscles and wandering hands and-

Focus, Maddie.

"See, Maddie's form here." Damian's hands hover over my hips, close but not quite touching. It's maddening, like a phantom caress, and I have to bite my lip to keep from leaning back into him.

I thought I had it down, mimicking his stance to a T. But apparently, my T needs some adjusting. Story of my life.

"I'd love to have her form," Aunt Locelli chimes in, and suddenly the room is abuzz with chatter. The women aged sixty-five to eighty-eight start swapping stories about how their perimenopause started years earlier (some in their early forties), how their menopause was different than what they expected, and things no one told them about.

And did I hear that vaginal atrophy isn't a joke?

It doesn't sound like a joke.

And hearing the way they're all chatting away like this means so much to them makes me itch to do more research.

To bring more awareness to these problems. Make them more accessible. And for at least a few seconds, I don't focus on Damian's scar on his face, the one that makes my heart take a bubble bath in my chest.

It makes me want to dig deeper, to shine a light on these issues that affect so many but are so rarely discussed.

I make a mental note to follow up on this later, to see if there's a story here worth pursuing. I can feel the itch to investigate, to report, thrumming under my skin. It's almost enough to distract me from the heat of Damian's body, the measured cadence of his breath. Almost.

But for now, my attention is inexorably drawn back to the man behind me as he shifts, his chest brushing against my back for the briefest of moments, and all thoughts of journalistic pursuits fly right out of my head. I'm hyperaware of every point of contact, every whisper of friction between us.

My gaze snags on the scar on his face, the one that cuts through his eyebrow and down his cheek. It's a mark of survival, of resilience, and it makes something in my chest clench. I want to trace it with my fingers, to learn the story behind it, to map out all the parts of him that make him whole.

I imagine pulling him into the locker room, shoving him against the wall. I'd press myself against him, feel every inch of his hard body against mine. My hands would roam over his chest, his abs, dipping lower and lower until I'm cupping him through his shorts...

I wonder if I could bring him to his knees with my mouth wrapped around his hard length. Or maybe he'd take control, hoist me up onto the sink, push my legs apart, and-

"Maddie? Did you hear me?"

Damian's voice jolts me out of my fantasy, and I pray to every deity I know that I'm not as flushed as I feel.

"Sorry, what was that?" I ask, hoping he'll attribute my breathlessness to the workout and not to the X-rated thoughts running through my head.

He smirks, like he knows exactly where my mind was at. "I said, let's try that move again. And this time... try to focus."

Right. Focus. Easier said than done with six feet of solid muscle pressed up against me, but I'll give it my best shot.

After all, there'll be plenty of time for fantasies later, when I'm alone in my bed with my trusty vibrator.

For now, I've got a class to get through. And a very fine ass to stare at—I mean, a very informative class to pay attention to.

Let's just hope I don't spontaneously combust before it's over.

But with Damian's heat seeping into me, his scent invading my senses, his eyes tracking my every move?

Let's just say, it's going to be a long, hard session.

And not in the way I'd like.

CHAPTER 20—DAMIAN

Alessandro: Maddie's podcast may be magic. I officially crunched some more numbers with the bank—and we might keep swimming. Especially as I know you're acing this class right now.

WATCHING MADDIE INTERACT with the class, I find myself doing a threat assessment out of habit. But the only threat here is to my own carefully constructed defenses. Abort mission, soldier. This is not a drill.

After helping her with her form, I've left Maddie to her own devices. Oh, I coached her from far away, but there's only so much thinking about the smell of week-old gym socks can achieve. I can't let myself get distracted by how much I want her. This is a self-defense class, not a chance to indulge my fantasies.

"Alright, ladies, listen up. Age is just a number, and these moves? They don't discriminate. Some of your bodies might not move like they used to, but neither do most of the punks you'd be defending against." I pause, showing them how to knee their opponent. "Let's work with what we've got."

"My wit?" Aunt Locelli says, matter-of-fact.

"Definitely your wit," I confirm. "And your body."

"Mine is roaring!" Miss Richardson chimes in.

"Mine is ready to bloom," Miss Hartwell adds with a wink.

The ladies dissolve into giggles, and I can't help but smile. Their enthusiasm is contagious.

I plant myself in the center, eyeing the group like I'm picking my squad for a high-stakes op. "Alright, who's brave enough to be my crash test dummy?"

Five of the ladies step forward, eagerness shining in their eyes. Maddie inches back, like she's worried I might single her out. Not a chance. I'm barely holding on to my control as it is.

"Mrs. Richardson." I nod at her, noting the determination in her stance. She's been one of the most dedicated students, always pushing herself.

As I guide Mrs. Richardson through the moves, showing the group how to use their height to their advantage, she leans in close. "Thank you for this," she whispers. "We've been needing this time altogether. We'll definitely be back."

Her words hit me square in the chest. This is why I do what I do. Why I push myself day in and day out. To give people the tools to protect themselves. To make sure no one else ends up like... well, like me.

I swallow past the sudden lump in my throat and give Mrs. Richardson a small nod. She smiles, understanding shining in her eyes, and rejoins the group.

I take a deep breath, forcing my attention back to the task at hand. Back to being the teacher, the protector. And if my gaze strays to Maddie more than it should, well... I'll just have to think about those damn gym socks a little harder.

THE GYM'S HEAVY WITH sweat and something else—Maddie's scent. It's like a security breach in my senses, and I'm inhaling deeper before I can stop myself. I focus on wiping down the mats, a routine task to ground me. But it's like trying to ignore a flashing red alert—pointless.

Maddie's working the room like she's gathering intel, firing off questions, and scribbling notes. Her face is flushed, her hair damp and clinging to her neck. My fingers itch to brush it aside, to check her pulse—purely professional, of course. Except there's nothing professional about wanting to taste the salt on her skin.

I clock a few of the ladies giving Maddie the cold shoulder as they leave, muttering and shaking their heads. My jaw clenches, protective instincts kicking in hard. They're reading the situation all wrong. They don't see past her tough exterior, don't realize it's just another form of self-defense. But I do. And that's a liability I can't afford.

"They only heard what you said at the crab feast—not the apology." Aunt Locelli's voice yanks me out of my thoughts. She's eyeing me with that look that says she's about to meddle. "It's like those viral moments that have a correction—but no one sees the correction."

I grunt, not trusting myself to form actual words. Aunt Locelli pats my arm, and it's both comforting and unsettling as hell, like she's got X-ray vision into my skull.

"I'll let you two discuss the class," she says, her tone dripping with suggestion. Then to Maddie, "You can tell Ed to quote me. This is exactly what we needed. Just to feel more confident. And to do something together." She pauses, a mischievous glint in her eye. "Also, we've got a bet going at the poker club: lovers?"

Maddie and I both let out a laugh that sounds like we're choking on gravel. "Definitely not lovers!" We blurt out in perfect sync, our voices hitting a pitch that'd make dogs wince. Then, we're suddenly finding everything else in the room fascinating.

"Mm-hmmm." Aunt Locelli's got that wide-I-know-something grin as she squeezes Maddie's shoulder on her way out. I can practically see the cogs turning in her head. No doubt she'll be flooding the Swans Cove group page with updates. I'll have a waitlist by sunrise.

"So..." Maddie's voice is aiming for casual, but there's a breathy quality to it that makes my pulse kick into overdrive. "That was something."

"Something good?" I reply, my eyes doing a slow sweep of her figure. Bad move. Now I'm all too aware of how her gym clothes hug every curve. I need a distraction. Maybe I should reorganize the equipment room or plan next week's class. Anything to ignore how her scent makes me want to toss every single one of my rules out the window.

"Definitely," she smiles, and that smile... it's like a punch to the gut. Sweet and sharp all at once. I clench my hands into fists, fighting the urge to reach out and touch her.

Instead, I step away, needing some distance. The air between us feels charged, dangerous. I run a hand through my hair, trying to regain my composure.

"So, uh," I clear my throat, searching for neutral ground. "How's the next portrait coming along? Ed seemed pretty excited about it."

She shrugs, her smile fading slightly. "It's... good. It's coming. You know how it is with deadlines."

I nod, even though I don't really know. An uncomfortable silence stretches between us. Finally, I can't help but ask the question that's been nagging at me.

"Heard you're skipping town soon," I manage, the words coming out rougher than I intended.

“Yep.” She pops the ‘p,’ her lips pursing in a way that makes me want to trace them with my thumb. Or my tongue. Or more.

“Swans Cove not living up to expectations?”

“Nope.”

She’s throwing my own short answers back at me, and it’s driving me crazy. I want to step closer, break through that cool exterior she’s putting up. I want to see her eyes flash, hear her voice rise. I want to push until she pushes back, until we’re both...

Damn it. I’m supposed to be keeping my distance. Guarding myself. But with Maddie? It’s like trying to hold back a tidal wave with my bare hands.

I study her, trying to figure out her angle. “So, what’s the real story? You’re here, attending class, but not chasing some fluff piece?”

She shifts like she’s uncomfortable in her own skin. “Ed’s bright idea. Wants me to live, and I quote, ‘the Swans Cove experience.’ That maybe it will help me be more attuned to people, myself, my stories.”

I grunt, turning that over in my head. I can't help but think about her podcast, the one with Ryan. Her voice got to me, made me hit replay more times than I want to admit. And that article about CASAs? Felt like a punch to the solar plexus.

Part of me wants to tell her. Let her know how her words burrowed under my skin, made me see her in a different light.

"Caught your podcast," I say, rubbing the back of my neck. "The Ryan one. It was... not what I expected."

Her eyes go wide for a second, surprise written all over her face. "You actually listened?"

I shrug, trying to play it cool and probably failing spectacularly. "Hard to miss when it's all anyone in this town can talk about."

She rolls her eyes, but there's a ghost of a smile on her lips. It does something to me I'm not ready to name.

"And?" she prompts, tilting her head. "What did the great Damian Mack think of my humble little podcast?"

I hesitate, caught between wanting to compliment her work and maintaining my guard. "It was... insightful. You've got a way of getting people to open up."

"That's kind of the point of journalism," she says, her tone a mix of pride and defensiveness.

I raise my hands up. "Okay. If you say so... and look," I start again, not sure where I'm going with this. "We both know you've got one foot out the door, but-"

"But what?" she challenges, eyes flashing. "You think I'm here to exploit your story? To dig up dirt on the local hero?"

I wince, memories flooding back. "Wouldn't be the first time. There was this blogger who was a fan of the entire Bonnie and Clyde persona my progenitors had going on. And he tried to find me when I was a teenager, always trying to snap photos, speculating about my past-"

"Stop," Maddie cuts in, her voice sharp. "I get it, okay? You've been burned before. But you can't keep projecting that onto every reporter you meet."

Her words hit a nerve, and I can see I've touched one of hers too. Her jaw is set, eyes blazing with a mix of hurt and determination.

"I'm not some vulture circling for a story," she continues, her voice tight. "I have ethics, I have standards." But it sounds like she's trying to convince herself as much as she's trying to convince me. "I made mistakes, sure. I mean, one of them went viral. And I put someone I respected in the middle of all of it, too."

"Did you tell him that?" I interject.

"I did. Just because I'm ambitious doesn't mean-" She stops abruptly, taking a deep breath. When she speaks again, her tone is controlled, almost icy. "And there's a difference between *Not-Crabby-News* and *Not-So-Crabby-News*," she says, cocking her hip in a way that short-circuits my brain.

"I noticed." I breathe out. "And like I said with the flowers, I'm sorry."

Her expression softens for a moment before hardening again. "How'd you know tulips were my favorite?"

I shrug. "Saw it online."

Her eyes narrow. "Where exactly?"

I hesitate, knowing I'm treading on thin ice. "It was in the comments section of an article about your... um, proposal."

Maddie's face goes pale, then flushes with anger. "You googled me?"

"I didn't go looking for it," I defend, even as I know it's a weak excuse. "It popped up as I was scrolling, preparing for the class."

"Right," she scoffs, her voice dripping with sarcasm. "I'm sure you just happened to stumble upon the most humiliating moment of my life while preparing for your not-so-seniors' self-defense class."

I wince, realizing how it sounds. "Look, I was curious. You're new in town, and-"

"And what?" she cuts in, her eyes blazing. "You thought you'd dig up some dirt on the city girl? Get some ammunition? I thought you already had enough on me because of that article I didn't even write."

"That's not-" I start, but she's on a roll.

"So you used techniques you find reprehensible for your own ends." She crosses her arms, fire dancing in her eyes.

"Never claimed to be a saint." I step closer. "But at least I'm upfront about my methods."

Her eyebrow arches. "What's that supposed to mean?"

"It means you're here, playing at small-town reporter, but we both know you're just passing through. Collecting stories like souvenirs."

"You don't know anything about my work or my intentions," she snaps.

"Don't I? Seems pretty clear to me, Princess."

The nickname slips out before I can stop it. Her gaze hardens to steel.

"Don't call me that."

Her lips purse in a pout that I'm dying to taste.

"What's the matter? Afraid the nickname might stick?" I taunt, unable to help myself.

She scoffs, her eyes blazing. "Please. I've dealt with far worse than some small-town tough guy with a hero complex who's too busy protecting people to deal with his own issues."

That hits a nerve I didn't even know I had. I take another step, invading her space. "Hero complex? That's rich coming from the big city journalist slumming it for a feel-good story."

"Is that all you got? You don't know me," she snaps, not backing down an inch.

"I know enough," I growl. "Tell me, Madison Smith, isn't that what you really want? To be worshipped, put on a pedestal?"

Maddie's eyes flash, her cheeks flushing. "You certainly don't know a damn thing about what I want," she hisses, jabbing a finger into my chest.

I catch her wrist, feeling her pulse race beneath my fingers. "Oh, I think I do," I growl, tugging her closer. "I think you want to be seen. Really seen. Not as the Ice Princess or the fallen reporter. Just Maddie."

She stares up at me, breathing hard, eyes dark. Waiting for my next move. For a second, I think she might storm off. Part of me wants her to. Anything to break this tension. But another part, the part I'm trying desperately to ignore, wants her to stay right where she is.

"Fuck you," she whispers, but there's no bite to it. Just raw vulnerability. It hits me harder than I expected.

Maddie's eyes flicker with something—uncertainty, desire, maybe both. She bites her lower lip, a habit I've noticed when she's deep in thought. "This is a bad idea," she mutters, almost to herself. "Such a bad idea."

Despite her words, her body inches closer as if drawn by some invisible force. We're suspended in this moment, both aware of the explosive potential between us.

Then, with agonizing slowness, her free hand comes up. Her fingers graze my jaw, feather-light and tentative. For a heartbeat, I think she might actually kiss me. But then she traces the scar on my cheek, her touch barely perceptible.

I suppress a shiver at her caress, my breath catching. The warmth of her fingers ignites something primal in me, and it takes all my willpower not to crush her against me.

I lean in close, my lips nearly brushing her ear. "You've been thinking about it, haven't you?" I rasp. "About me. About us."

She shivers, not pulling away. "You're insufferable," she breathes, pressing closer to me.

"Am I?" I challenge, my hand sliding to her hip. "Prove me wrong, then. Walk away."

She doesn't move. Just stares at me, conflict clear in her eyes.

"That's what I thought," I murmur. "So stop talking and do something about it."

Something snaps between us. With a muttered "Fuck it," she surges forward. I'm there to meet her, no hesitation. This isn't gentle. It's all teeth and tongue, a clash as fierce as our argument.

My hand fists in her hair, angling her head just so. She bites my lower lip hard enough to sting, and I growl low in my throat. She's like wildfire in my arms.

I walk her back against the wall, my thigh wedging between her legs. She grinds down, shameless and needy, and I can feel the heat of her even through our clothes. Fuck me, she feels good.

"I hate you," she pants against my mouth, but her fingers are digging into my shoulders, pulling me closer.

"Liar," I rasp, trailing bruising kisses along her jaw, down her throat. She arches into me, and I swear I could get drunk on the little sounds she's making. "You want this. You want me."

"One moment," she breathes, her nails raking down my back. "That's all this is."

I smile against her skin, my teeth grazing her pulse point. "Whatever you say..." I refrain the urge to call her Princess because she's made it clear she doesn't want me to, but I'm going to make sure she feels like one right now.

Then I'm kissing her again, pouring all my frustration and longing into the slide of our tongues. The world narrows down to the heat of her body, the taste of her, the little mewling sounds she makes in the back of her throat.

Tomorrow, I'll probably regret this. My rules are there for a reason, dammit. But with Maddie in my arms, her fingers working their way south, those rules seem like a distant memory. Fuck it. Some bridges are worth burning.

I'm done fighting this. Done pretending. I want her, simple as that.

And for this moment, she's mine.

And I intend to make every second count.

CHAPTER 21—MADDIE

Subject line: Thank you for your submission
Dear Madison Smith, Thank you for submitting to Not-So-Crabby News in the "Small-Town Articles to Make People Smile" category, which opens twice a year. If you advance, you could win a worldwide tour to report on all the happy news you see. Results will be announced next week.
Stay Not Crabby,
Not-So-Crabby News Team

MY BODY AND BRAIN ARE in open rebellion, both screaming for more. More of him. Pretty sure this isn't what Ed meant by "experiencing Swans Cove." Unless the town's motto is "Come for Maryland's Eastern shore's charm, stay for the potentially mind-blowing orgasms. No Old Bay needed."

"It's a mistake," I mutter, the words slipping out before I can stop them.

Damian freezes, his body going rigid against mine. His calloused hands, still splayed across my back, twitch slightly. I can feel the heat of his breath on my neck as he tilts back just enough to look at me.

"A mistake?" he growls, his voice low and dangerous. There's a flash of something in his eyes—hurt? anger?—before it's masked by a steely resolve. "I'm no one's mistake."

I open my mouth to respond, then close it again. My brain is short-circuiting, caught between the lingering taste of him on my lips and the alarm bells ringing in my head.

"Well..." I start, then falter. Come on, Maddie. Words are your thing. Use them.

I take a deep breath, acutely aware of every point where our bodies are still touching. "Well, it was a good kiss, you know. Technically speaking." I lick my lips, remembering. "But still a mistake."

He doesn't need to know that this kiss seems to have the butterflies racing down a newly minted F1 track with his name on it.

But after a few seconds, the infuriating man lifts the corner of his lips like I've poked the bear—a very impressive bear. His green eyes zero in on me and why, oh, why do I want to shift on my feet?

Instead, I raise an eyebrow, challenging him.

Wrong move.

The electricity crackling through the air could power the entire State of Maryland. Probably the entire universe. "Technically speaking?" His finger tucks a strand of my curly hair behind my ear and grazes my rose tattoo. I'd like to present the goosebumps scattering across my skin as evidence that this is a bad idea.

I don't lose control. Not like that. And yet, I'm inching toward him as if I can't get close enough.

Reminder to self: I'm angry. Pissed. Furious. Really upset.

"As I said, I'm no one's mistake," he rasps out, and there's a world of hurt in those words, those eyes, that voice. "You decide..." I half-expect him to call me Princess again. I half-want him to.

"I'm leaving. That's why you want this," I murmur, and I have to remind myself that the fact I'm going to race out of town, leaving Swans Cove in the rearview mirror, is the only reason I want this.

Damian is not part of the plan.

"Maybe," he groans. "You're driving me wild. I want to make you lose control. Shit, Mads, I want to lose control."

My heart shouldn't stutter at him calling me Mads—like he cares. Like I'm special. Like those four little letters actually mean something.

Plus, hearing that he wants to lose control? I know how much that must have taken him for him to say that. Because I understand him.

And I kiss him again. More tenderly at first. Taking my time. Brushing my hand on his strong back, underneath his shirt. His torso is hard. His... everything is hard.

His finger now traces my jaw, and am I leaning into him? Yep. Yep, I am.

This is how Anthony must have felt in Bridgerton. The push and pull. The undeniable attraction to someone you really shouldn't be attracted to.

I don't even like the guy.

I don't like him. He's too sure of himself. Too loud. Too... perceptive.

"It's true I don't do relationships," he growls, and those words shouldn't sound hollow in my chest. "And you want to leave anyways." He reminds himself or me.

I am leaving.

Going. Gone. Goner.

I cross my fingers he doesn't glance down because I'm pretty sure my nipples are straining against my shirt, and if his hand continued down, down, down, he would feel how much my body is reacting to his.

Chemicals.

Nothing more.

And maybe that's something we need to get out of our system. It's not like having sex with the man will get me attached to him—we're not swans or penguins—and it's been forever since I felt wanted.

My gaze flits down, and my face flushes. He definitely wants me.

"I don't do relationships either." And for good measure, I add. "And I'm still mad at you."

"Angry sex can be good." Damian's voice drops to a low growl as he braces one arm against the wall beside my head, effectively caging me in. His other hand hovers near my hip, not quite touching anymore but close enough that I can feel the heat radiating from his skin. "Furious, no-holding-back sex?" He leans in, his lips barely grazing my ear as he whispers, "Even better."

"Mmm-hmmm." Inhale, Maddie. Don't forget to breathe. "One moment. You and I. Just one moment. Now. Actually, just now."

Damian doesn't laugh like I dreaded he would. Oh no, he doesn't laugh. Doesn't even smile. The intensity in his gaze amps up as his fingers trace the tattoo on my neck.

I'm not going to lose control. I'm not going to lose myself. But something in his eyes, a flicker of warmth beneath the desire, makes me hesitate. This man has me teetering on the edge of a precipice I've spent decades avoiding. It's like his green eyes see right through all my defenses, my carefully crafted image, my desperate need to prove myself. And that makes me want to go *weeee*—like I'm on a rollercoaster—or hide... somewhere. Most likely in a dark movie theater playing a Scream marathon.

So, maybe it's self-preservation kicking in, or maybe it's a test. Either way, the words are out before I can stop them.

"They called me the Ice Princess." I hold my breath, watching his reaction.

Part of me is hoping he'll take the bait, use this as an excuse to walk away. It would be easier that way, wouldn't it? No messy feelings, no complications. Just two ships passing in the night.

But the words keep coming, like a dam breaking. "It started in middle school. I was always the girl with the perfect grades, the flawless presentation. Never a hair out of place, never a moment of weakness." I laugh, but it comes out bitter. "God forbid I show any emotion. One day, I didn't cry when I bombed a test. I didn't cry when the teacher used my essay—*my essay*—as an example on what not to do. And they started writing notes about me on the bathroom stalls. My locker. Took my notebooks and left me mean messages." I shake my head. I showed that teacher. All of them. "I still didn't cry. Not in front of them. And suddenly, I was the Ice Princess.

Cold. Unfeeling. It stuck all the way through college, through my career, through my boyfriends." I swallow hard. "That nickname... it still stings. Makes me feel like I'm always one step away from freezing everyone out."

That has him raising an eyebrow. We were talking about sex, and now I'm unloading years of emotional baggage. I half-expect him to whirl around, to tell me he doesn't need my pity stories. That they're nothing. That I should get a grip. My heart thumps in my ears, waiting for his answer, torn between hoping he'll stay and praying he'll go.

"I'm sorry." He sounds like he means it, too. His brow furrows, and for a moment, he looks away. When he meets my eyes again, there's a rawness there I haven't seen before. "My parents stopped writing to me when I no longer served a purpose to them. They called me the Lost Boy."

Forget thumping, my heart breaks for him. The gym suddenly feels too small, too intimate. I'm acutely aware of our breathing, the faint hum of the air conditioning, the lingering scent of disinfectant.

He continues, his voice low and intense, "The Ice Princess? Maddie, please." He shakes his head, a small smile playing at the corners of his mouth. "You're hotter than lava."

I can't help but snort at that, and his smile widens.

"And I'm not only talking about your body, your curves, your smile..." He inches closer, and I fight the urge to step back, to maintain some semblance of control. His fingers trail down my back, sending shivers across my skin. "I'm talking about the way you laugh, the way you care about the stories you tell and the people around you. About Fluffy, about the way you move, the way you kissed me..."

"You kissed me too," I whisper, and this time, there's a hint of a smile on his lips.

"I did, didn't I?" he rasps out, and I don't think I realized until now how a voice can be sexy. Like toe-curling sexy because my toes are definitely curling.

"You did," I murmur as his hand roams lower, skimming over my waist, my hips, and it would appear my lungs have stopped working correctly because I'm holding my breath until he pulls me flush against him, and I let out a sigh. I can feel the evidence of his desire pressing against me, and a shiver runs through my entire body.

He must feel it because he gives me a knowing smile and leans forward. His lips nibble my ear as I'm holding on to him like he's a raft in a storm, and with his breath hot on my skin, he growls, "And I'm going to kiss you again." His teeth nibble the sensitive skin of my neck, and my fingers clutch to his broad shoulders. "I'm going to devour you, taste you, and have you lose all control..."

"I... I don't lose control," I utter, and it's like I issued him a challenge.

"Oh, you will."

"I...im-po-ssible."

"Do you want to?" He asks, and how is it that him asking that question in that growly voice of his when I can already tell he's holding himself back has me melting for him?

"Yes."

"Thank fucking you," he grunts, and his mouth crashes onto mine as he tugs me closer again against his hard chest, his hard body, his hard... everything. He smells like sweat and just him. A scent that I want to bottle for those winter days coming up. When his tongue slides against mine, he tastes of coffee and mint and pure desire. His fingers dig into my waist, and even with holding on to him, I still feel out of balance—but for once, it doesn't feel like the end of the world.

One of my hands reaches up to his hair while he deepens the kiss, and I rub myself against him, wanting—no, needing to feel him even closer. To feel him inside of me.

When he breaks the kiss, he rasps out. "Just now you said?"

I nod.

"No more than that, and then we go our separate ways."

"We don't work together ever again—I'll see you in the hallway, and I'll wave. Nothing more." I pause. "I'll complain about your music and the noise. And the laundry."

"And I'll get annoyed by your know-it-all attitude." His fingers now trail up my yoga pants, and even though there's fabric between his touch and my skin, I can feel it. All of it. "But right now? Right now, I'm going to know exactly how you taste before fucking you so hard you'll remember this moment for years to come."

My mouth dries up, and I try to utter something, anything which only comes out as "Ghm."

"You were saying?"

"Promise?"

"I fucking swear it. And you know my word means everything."

He slowly undresses me, groaning almost in pain as his eyes feast on my body.

"Beautiful," he whispers in awe, and his lips trail down my collarbone to my nipple.

He blows over it, waking up nerves I didn't remember even existed, and when he starts sucking and nibbling and licking while his fingers trace some pattern on my stomach on their way to my very core, I moan, "Damian."

He glances up at me with a feral look that dries up my throat. This man wants me.

All of me. And he groans, "That's right. I'm the one who makes you lose control." When I whimper again, his smile is downright feral. "Good girl."

I'd protest that I'm nobody's good girl, but for some reason, hearing him say it like this has me wanting to nod, to do anything to have him keep going. Luckily, he doesn't wait, his lips close around my other nipple, and his fingers find their way to my very core, teasing me.

Slowly, Damian sinks to his knees, his hands trailing down my body as he goes. He lifts one of my legs over his shoulder, opening me up to him. I glance to our left, catching our reflection in the full-length mirror near the equipment rack. The sight of us—him on his knees, me against the wall with my fingers tangled in his hair—sends another jolt of desire through me.

I'm flushed. My mouth gaping open, and bucking my hips toward him, I've never felt more beautiful.

And when one of his fingers curls into me, I gasp. "I can smell you," he whispers. "And man, you smell delicious. Can't wait to see how you taste." His breath ghosts over my most sensitive area, sending shivers up my spine. "You've been waiting, haven't you?" But he's not looking up at me. He's staring straight ahead.

"Are you talking to..." I can barely form words, my brain short-circuiting from his proximity.

"To the prettiest cunt ever? You bet. It's a piece of art." He places a gentle kiss just above where I need him most. "I think we should give it a name. How about...Venus? Hmmm, no. Too formal. That doesn't work. Pr..." I half-expect him to say Princess again like an old habit he can't quit, and my shoulders tighten ever-so-slightly. He must notice it because he pauses, his eyes flicking up to mine.

"Peach—-and he adds... y... Peachy."

"Like Princess Peach?" A snort of laughter bursts out of me despite the aching need pulsing through my core. "Princess Peach-y?"

And my laughter turns into full-blown giggles.

"I wasn't sure... Princess was the right term after what you said... but Princess Peach did cross my mind." He chuckles, a warm sound that makes my heart flutter.

For the first time, being called Princess feels... different. Intense in the best way. "Princess Peachy," I murmur. "Are you seriously naming my..."

"Hey now," he growls playfully, his stubble grazing my inner thigh. "Show some respect. We're in the presence of a real Princess here. Royalty even. And she's fucking beautiful."

The nickname rolls off his tongue with such ease, and there's no hint of mockery—only affection and playful reverence. It's as if he's reclaiming it, transforming it into something beautiful.

I'm caught between laughing and moaning as he plants feather-light kisses along my folds. "No one... no one has ever talked to me like that."

His eyes, dark with desire, meet mine. "Well, sweetheart, I'm about to say—and do—a lot of things no one's ever done before. Now, I need to know if Princess Peach-y tastes as sweet as she looks. Call it a service to the kingdom."

It's like he's on a mission with his tongue, each lick and swirl sending shockwaves through me. I clutch his shoulders, probably hard enough to leave marks. Sorry, definitely not sorry. His large fingers—one, then two—curl inside me, and I swear I can feel them from the top of my head to my manicured toes.

A tidal wave builds low in my belly, growing with each pass of his tongue, with each thrust of his fingers, with his teeth grazing my clit. It's too much and not enough all at once. I want more. I want to pull him so much closer. I want... I want...

"Damian!" His name tears from my throat as the wave crashes over me. I'm seeing stars, fireworks, maybe even a comet. It's like every cell in my body tingles, high-fives each other, and jumps up and down.

As I float back down to earth, turned into a buzzing jellyfish, I hear his gravelly voice. "Oh, I'm not done with you, love."

I crack open an eye to see him standing, looking like the cat that got the cream. And wow, when did he lose his pants? My eyes go wide, ping-ponging between his face and his, um, very impressive anatomy, that's demanding attention. I'm tempted to salute him. I lick my lips.

"Keep looking at me like that..." he growls, and I swear I can feel the heat of his gaze.

I reach out, tracing a finger along him. He shudders, and a little thrill zips through me. I did that. Me. Madison "Ice

Princess" Smith, making the Greek God with tattoos and scars and that half-grin quiver. Take that, high school nicknames.

"I wish I could feel your lips on me. Your tongue..." he whispers, like he's sharing a secret. "But if you do, I'll explode right there. And I need to be inside you."

All I can manage is another embarrassing "Ghm." Smooth, Maddie. Really eloquent. A Pulitzer-worthy utterance right there.

We slide to the floor, and the cool mat jolts me back to reality. I'm about to have sex. In a gym. With my insanely hot neighbor. The one I hate and am totally mad at. Right?

"Always prepared," he murmurs as he fumbles for a condom from his sweatpants, then pauses. His eyes roam over me, and I resist the urge to cover up. "But I don't think I was ever prepared for you. Do you know how perfect you are?"

His gaze catches on my phoenix tattoo, matching his own. Something shifts in his eyes,. a flash of... recognition? Understanding? For a moment, it feels like he really sees me. All of me.

I look away. Don't go there, Maddie. This is just sex. Really hot, definitely not life-altering sex. His dick is not a magic wand... oh.... But maybe it is.

"Just now," I whisper, more to myself than to him. A reminder. A promise. A lie?

Then he's inside me, stretching me, filling me in a way that has me gasping. My nails dig into his back like they're coming home as I wrap my legs around him. The weight of him, the feel of him... it's ... good. So. Good.

"Okay, Peachy," he rasps out. "Just now."

And then he moves, and all coherent thought flies out the window. Who needs thinking anyway? Thinking is overrated when you're—oh yes, right there—about to have your second mind-blowing orgasm of the night.

Just for now.

Right. Keep telling yourself that, Maddie.

No broken heart. No strings attached.

Because I'm leaving Swans Cove.

At least, that's what I keep on telling myself as I slip out of the gym, my legs still wobbly and my heart racing. One moment. That's all it is.

A WEEK LATER.

But one moment has a funny way of stretching into days, then a week. And here I am, seven days later, still feeling the ghost of his touch on my skin. Not replaying every memory from the gym shouldn't be that hard. Ha! "Hard."

Great choice of words, brain. Now I'm picturing Damian's abs and... um, everything else that's oh so impressive. My body's apparently decided to produce a whole documentary titled "The Damian Experience: A Hands-On Study." Coming soon to an icy cold shower near you.

I'm deep into my millionth Scream rewatch—because nothing says "I'm totally over that hot guy," like watching people get stabbed—when my phone pings. For a nanosecond, my heart does this weird flippy thing, hoping it's a "Hey, Princess, want to come downstairs?" from Mr. Muscles and Orgasms.

Princess. Huh. The word that used to make me want to hurl my laptop at the nearest wall now bounced around in my head like a Formula One car on a victory lap. Warm. Playful. For the first time, it didn't feel like a slap in the face or a dare to prove myself.

In Damian's growly voice, it was almost... sweet? Nope. Not going there. But maybe... okay, fine. Maybe it was a tiny bit affectionate. A far cry from the ice-cold crown I'd been trying to shatter for years. Maybe being a "princess," especially "Princess Peach-y" isn't all about perfection or living up to what I believe is everyone else's fairy tale expectations. I shake my head, biting back a laugh. Two mind-blowing orgasms, and I'm waxing poetic on princesses. And peaches. Get it together, Maddie.

I grab my phone and scroll down the notification. But it's not Damian. Nope, it's something else entirely.

Not-So-Crabby-News results.

My fingers find my heart necklace, fiddling with it like it's some sort of magic 8-ball that'll tell me whether to open the email or not. I want to win. I'm going to win. There's no universe where Madison Smith doesn't win this thing. It's practically written in the stars. Or at least it better be, because leaving town has been the master plan all along. I'm 110% ready for the next big step in my career. Because Swans Cove can't be my final destination.

Damian and I aren't a thing. We'll never be a thing. So heartbreak would be waiting. And I've got enough of those.

Okay, and maybe a few more earth-shattering, toe-curling, seeing-stars orgasms.

But definitely heartbreak.

That's my story, and I'm sticking to it.

Dear Madison Smith,

Thank you for your entry in Not-So-Crabby-News. While we think your entry has plenty of potential, a crab feast seems too on the nose for this prize. Our judges would love for you to enter with another story during the holiday season...

Looking forward to it,

The Not-So-Crabby-News Team.

My eyes scan the email, and I wince so hard I'm pretty sure my face did a full gymnastics routine. Looks like I'm stuck in Swans Cove a bit longer... if Ed agrees, that is.

The music from downstairs suddenly cranks up to eleven because, of course it does. Damian's doing, no doubt. As memories of our... ahem, "workout" in the gym come flooding back again, I feel my cheeks flush hotter than the lava cake at Plates & Drinks.

What have I gotten myself into? This wasn't part of the script. I'm supposed to be the cool, collected reporter breezing through town, not the rom-com heroine falling for the local grumpy hottie. But here I am, feeling like I've just stepped onto the set of my own personal Hallmark movie.

Except this one's definitely rated R.

I glance back at the screen as Fluffy cuddles up to me. Even Sidney Prescott, with what feels like her seven lives, would be out of her depth here.

...Right?

DISCOVER WHAT HAPPENS to Maddie and Damian in # Dear Santa, With Love[1]...The Christmas Spicy Romcom to make you smile and swoon. Start reading now[2]... And you can, of course, get a bonus scene by joining my newsletter[3] (if you haven't already😊).

And don't forget to leave a review[4], spread the word, share on socials... Everything is OH. SO. APPRECIATED. Thank you.

---

1. https://books2read.com/dearsantawithlove
2. https://books2read.com/dearsantawithlove
3. https://subscribepage.io/9EuZte
4. https://books2read.com/u/bp9ayz

Acknowledgments

DEAR YOU,

Yes, you, reading this novel all the way to the acknowledgments. This one is for you.

I'm writing these with *Virgin River* in the background, Plato the Dog sleeping on the couch next to me, The Chemical Engineer working out, and Bobbie Voltaire the Cat snoozing away... waiting for the moment I try to rest to come meow that he really should be carried back upstairs.

I've been writing novels for decades, really. Professionally speaking, it's been ten years this year in 2024. As I write, I think about the characters, what is true for them, their experience. And I think about you, dear reader. I'd like to thank you for reading this book, for picking it up, for maybe even falling in love with Maddie and Damian. Oh, how I hope this book made you smile. And I cross my fingers you continue loving them in *# Dear Santa, With Love.*

As always, I'm so very grateful to my wonderful and supportive husband, who continues to inspire me and make me laugh. Together, we grow. I can be myself with him, and that has informed a lot of my writing. My hope for all of you, whether it's with a partner or with a friend, a neighbor, a family member, is to have someone like this in your life. Also, he spends so much time finding the right reels to send to me just so that I smile. (I just read this out loud to him after he said, "I assume I'm in there," and he approves.)

To my family: while I sometimes write about the negative effects of social media, I also am SO thankful that this technology exists so that we can see each other much more often. I say it every time, but I'm so lucky that you are my family.

My tight circle of friends—you may be near and far, but know that your friendship means the world to me.

To Katy Upperman and Alison Miller: I am so lucky that I get to talk plotting and writing and life with you two. Can you believe that this little thing called blogging connected us all those years ago despite the miles? So. Thankful.

This one also goes to Leslye Penelope, Elsie Silver, and Darby Kane... Your books have helped me rediscover my love of reading right when I was too busy writing, writing, writing... Not only am I so happy I got to immerse myself in the stories you created, but you also made said-writing stronger without maybe even realizing it.

I don't think I'll ever write another book without thanking Dr. Aaron Rapoport and his team at The University of Maryland Marlene and Stewart Greenebaum Comprehensive Cancer Center—thank you for your expertise and kindness. Thank you for never making me feel like a number. Thanks to you, I'm living so many happy moments that will become cherished memories. And I'll continue to do so.

And then, because without her, my brain wouldn't have learned how to understand my OCD thinking patterns so that I could refrain from crossing the bridge into the story: thank you, Dr. Surbeck, for always continuing to learn so you could help me even more. Inference-based Cognitive Behavioral Therapy (i-CBT) has been incredibly helpful to me (in addition to ERP).

Writing can be solitary, but thanks to Becca Syme (and the Better, Faster Academy), I now have a virtual office and wonderful colleagues who make me laugh and are full of support and wisdom and also... very important facts (smiling remembering some of those very important facts).

And thank you again, dear reader, for taking a chance on me.

Wishing you so many smiles,

Elodie

About the copyeditor

KAEL PRYBLE: Kael has been a copyeditor for the past two years, primarily focusing on contemporary romance and romantasy. An avid lover of reading, they always have a book in hand, whether it's something they're reviewing for a passionate writer or something they're picking up for fun in their free time.

Email: Kaelpryble@gmail.com

About the author

AUTHOR PICTURE BY ELIZABETH Rogers

Elodie Nowodazkij writes sizzling rom-coms with grumpy book boyfriends and the bold, funny women who win their hearts. Sometimes, she even writes stories that scare the crap out of her. Raised in a small French village, she almost always had a book in her hands. At nineteen, she moved to the U.S., where she found out her French accent is here to stay. Now in Maryland with her husband, dog, and cat, she whips up heartwarming, hilarious, and hot romances. Ready to take the plunge? The water's delightfully warm.

Find Elodie online:

www.elodienowodazkij.com[1]

https://www.facebook.com/enowodazkij/
https://www.instagram.com/enowodazkij/
https://www.tiktok.com/@elodienowodazkij

1. http://www.elodienowodazkij.com

Printed in the USA
CPSIA information can be obtained
at www.ICGtesting.com
LVHW040347291024
795075LV00039B/811

9 798227 536372